THE HEART OF HADES

Jessica Congreve

contents

Prologue

Eighteen year old Namie Bakers shivered as the cold autumn breeze blew in, goosebumps forming on her arms and legs. She had decided to leave her friends' party early, seeing how she had an interview tomorrow and didn't want to go home blackout drunk, knowing her parents would scold her for such behavior. And knowing that all her friends were already hammered, she walked home, not bothering to call an Uber seeing how she had no money.

Besides, her home was only a few blocks away, and the neighborhood was secured and safe from robbers and assaulters, how bad could walking home be?

Such a naive little human.

Namie walked a little faster, wanting to hurry home and out of the cold weather. The cold was never her favorite about the autumn season, especially on how cold the nights were.

"I should've brought a jacket," the girl mumbled under her breath, rubbing her arms up and down for warmth.

It was then when she heard something snap behind her, a heavy boot snapping a stick in half. She froze for a moment, listening to see if someone was following her. Hearing no further footsteps, she waved it off as her paranoid imagination and continued home. But as she walked, the feeling of sutle dread clawed its way up her spine, leaving goosebumps under her shirt.

She stopped again, and looked over her shoulder to see if someone was following her. Of course, no one was there, not even a passing stray.

Feeling her paraonia grow, she quickly hurried onto her street, not looking back as she approached the safety of her home.

Namie sighed in relief as she was under the safety of the porch light, the dread now gone.

But as she stepped onto the porch, she heard the sound of a chuckle before freezing in mid-step. She didn't even register that the person behind her held a long kitchen knife in their hand. She turned around, and before she could scream, white hot pain exploded in her back as the stranger plunged the knife into her.

Up in the window facing the front lawn, her little sister of fourteen years, stared as she watched her older sister be killed in front of her eyes. She could not scream as the shock and fear prevented her from speaking. Namie gasped as she fell onto the cobblestone steps of the porch, dark crimson blood pooling around her.

Satisfied with their work, the person took the knife from the girl's back and looked up the window to see the younger sister staring at them. Under the hood, they couldn't help but smirk at the little girl's fear.

The stranger lifted up the knife and pointed it towards the girl, and before leaving, they mouthed; "You will be mine next."

CHAPTER 1: VOICES IN THE NIGHT

A stray tear rolled down Katherine Bakers pale cheek as she quietly grieved by her older sister's gravestone. The day was gray and dark and cold, but Katherine was use to the constant coldness.

It had been five years since her sister's murder. Five years of constant paranoia, nightmares, and socially detachment from the outside world. Most people would grieve and try to move on with their memories, but Katherine didn't.

Watching her bestest friend, her flesh and blood, be killed in front of her had shattered her, breaking any sense of safety for her as she awoke every night from her nightmare, thinking the man in the hoodie was there for her.

Katherine wiped away her stray tears as she laid the lilies—Namie's favorite flower—onto the damp earth on the grave. She silently read the words craved onto the head-stone:

"Though you were taken off this earth too soon, the people you've impacted will carry on your memory. In loving memory of Namie Winter Bakers."

Katherine couldn't help but smile sadly as she touched the cold stone. Namie hated the cold; today was nothing what she represented.

Getting up from her knees, she wiped the mud from her jeans, and walked out of the cemetery with the cold sweeping through her skin.

Over the last five years, Katherine had slowly began to recluse herself from the town. With the constant paranoia and lack of sleep, she had shut the outside world—including her family—out and stayed in the safety of her childhood room.

She reached home, seeing that neither of her parents were home. Since Namie's death, both of the girl's parents had buried themselves in drink and work, ignoring their only daughter as they'd grieve for the daughter they praised.

Though she didn't want to admit it, a small part of Katherine had hoped that the spotlight that shined on Namie would shift to her. All she wanted was the comfort of her mother after a nightmare, and the smile that her father once wore.

Through their childhood, Katherine was jealous of her older sister. Though she felt terrible for such thoughts, the ten and eleven year old Katherine Bakers was jealous of her perfect sister. Now, all she wanted was to go back and not take her sister for granted.

She stepped into the dark and cold house, the silence greeting her with open arms.

Katherine knew her parents won't be back tonight; her father at the office and her mother drunk and in another man's bed. She was use to this, it has been going on since she was fourteen.

The gray day slowly turned into an inky black night. Katherine had sent the day doing assignments from her professors and playing her music through the speakers.

Normally, Katherine would try to stay awake during the night in fear of new nightmares waiting for her, but the visit to Namie's grave took a toll on her.

Shutting off all the lights minus a few lamps, Katherine trudged upstairs to her room.

The room Katherine and Namie shared was a spacious room with royal purple walls and white furniture. On the right side was Katherine's side with a small bed in the corner, posters of movies and bands she enjoyed, and clothing scattered on the floor.

Namie's side was always neat and cleared of any signs of a mess. With books on her selves in line, bed neatly made, and everything organized to Namie's expectations.

Because Namie was the older sister, they had a pale curtain to divide their room for the sake of Namie being a teenager and wanting her privacy.

In the dim overhead light, her side of the room looked ghostly with a thin layer of dust on the surface. It was frozen in time, stuck in the past, waiting for her to come back.

Katherine walked over to her side of the room and quickly changed to leggings and a stained shirt. Her long black hair was fizzy from the mist during her visit and tangled up in large knots. Brushing it through, she braided it into a simple side braid.

Everyone always said she and Namie looked almost identical. Apart from the age gap, they did share the same black hair, vivid blue eyes, and pale skin. While Namie had more of an athletic build, Katherine had little curves and was petite for her age. She looked like a child.

"Not done that road again," Katherine whispered to herself. She didn't want to think of the negatives of her sister, it always brought up harbored feelings from her childhood.

Climbing into her bed, she curled up into the covers, silent tears running down her face.

Just when she was about to close her eyes, she heard someone whisper to her, saying her name over and over. At first, she thought it was her imagination, but when she continued to hear it, dread had made itself a home in the pit of her stomach.

"W-Who's there," she called out, only to have darkness and silence answer back.

"Katherine..." The voice was chilling and haunting, but yet, it was smooth and husky like they had just got out of bed. It was obviously a man's voice, but none of which Katherine knew of. It wasn't her father, and she certainly didn't know a lot of boys her age.

She carefully got out of bed and went to the window that overlooked the front lawn, and as if history was repeating, she saw a hooded figure standing in the grass under the tree.

Fear coursed through Katherine's veins as her eyes locked on with the stranger's. Her hands suddenly felt clamy as her heart beat grew faster, beating violently in her chest.

Through the shadows, she saw the stranger smirk, and slowly walked out from under the tree. Unlike five years ago, he held no knife, he just stood motionless with a smirk on his face.

He reached into his front pocket and retrieved a cell phone. The shadows of the hood made sure that the light would not allow Katherine to see the face of her sister's murderer. The stranger typed into the phone and put it back into his pocket.

Suddenly, Katherine's phone buzzed on her nightstand, signaling that she had a message.

In all her life, Katherine had never felt such fear as she looked at her phone before turning her attention back to the lawn, only to see the man was gone.

She quickly got back into bed with her cell phone clutched tightly in her grasp. She didn't know whether to look at the message on there or pretend that all of this was a nightmare.

She knew that it was no coincidence that she recieved a text the same time that the man had sent a text to someone else. But her curiosity got the better of her.

Curiosity killed the cat.

Opening up her messages, she saw that she received a text from an unknown number. Clicking on the message, her blood ran cold in horror as she stared at the glowing message.

"It has been a long time, Katherine. I do hope you've enjoyed the last five years I've gifted to you. But now, it is your turn, my little kitten."

CHAPTER 2

Katherine sat alone, like usual, at the kitchen island as she ate from the bowl.

After seeing that text, she had only slept for a few hours from the fear, but even those few hours, the nightmare was far worse than the previous ones.

She dreamt that the murderer had kidnapped her and took her to a place of only darkness. She screamed for her sister, mother, and father, but the man simply laughed as he said no one would come for her.

She had awoke in cold sweat with her stomach rolling. She barely made it to the bathroom where she vomited the little food she managed to eat the day before.

Now, she sat numb in her thoughts, paying no attention to the soggy cereal or the commotion from the living room. Katherine knew it was her mother coming home after spending the night in a strangers arms and drinking; she could smell the whiskey and the sex that radiated off that woman.

Rachelle Bakers, just like everyone else who lost a child, was grieving in her own way. As her husband Dean Bakers stayed at work, Rachelle had used the lack of attention from her husband and looked for much younger bachelors. Though the thought of a forty year old woman cheating on her husband with a nineteen year old sickened her, Katherine had no say on the matter.

Rachelle stumbled into the kitchen, her tight dress in tatters and her brown hair a rats nest, whiskey surrounding her.

Katherine covered her nose with the sleeve of her hoodie, trying not to smell the horrid scent of regret, shame, and way too many shots of tequila and whiskey.

Her mother spared her no glance as she opened up the wine cabinet and took a swig of the bitter liquor before stumbling back towards the stairs and up to her separate room.

After a few moments, Katherine took her hand off her mouth and took in a deep now that the scent of liquor was gone. It was rare for her to see her mother in the morning. Most times, Katherine would be upstairs in her room or her mother wouldn't come back at all; not that Dean Bakers really noticed, he practically lived in his office.

No longer hungry, she dumped the soggy cereal into the trash bin and decided to go out for a while. She rarely did go out, not including her visits to the grave. Today, she felt that she wanted to be alone without anyone.

Like yesterday, the sky was gray as a slight drizzle fell from the clouds above. Katherine didn't bother putting up her hood as the drizzle settled on her skin.

Brookside Mayne was a small and quiet town outside of Portland, Oregon. It was settled in the mountains which attracted many hikers and tourists in the summer and fall months.

It was the town that you could raise a family, where you didn't have to lock your doors. But after Namie's death, the town had sheltered itself.

Katherine ignored the passing looks of pity as she walked. Everyone was horrified and shocked to hear of the random murder, pitying the younger sister as she was the one to see her own flesh and blood die before her:

Katherine watched the stranger walk away from Namie's body after telling her that he will come for her.

Her voice was lodged in her throat; she couldn't scream for her parents. She just stood there.

Namie laid motionless on the steps of the front porch, blood dripping down onto the pathway and pooling around the body. In the darkness, the younger sister could see how Namie's skin had turned several shades paler under the veil of black hair.

She was able to move after a few long moments, and she quickly ran down the stairs and onto the porch.

Katherine starred at the dead body of her sister, watching the blood seep through her shirt and trailing down her sides. So much blood...

"Bad dream," Katherine whispered to herself, not wanting to face the crush reality in front if her. "T-This is just a bad dream. O-Or a prank... H-Haha, very funny Namie."

But unlike the previous times of joking and pranking each other, this time, it was no joke. Namie was dead.

"Come on, Namie, it's not funny anymore."

Katharine was careful to avoid the blood and sat next to her sister's body. She placed her hand on Namie's shoulder and shook it gently, like all the times she had to wake up her big sister.

She didn't even realize that tears were falling down her cheeks and splashing onto the cobblestone. Her shaking grew more harsh as she cried and wailed, the reality now settling in.

Her big sister was dead.

Katherine shook her head, ridding the memories of that night.

Reminding herself of that night made the open wounds stretch and bleed, causing her more grief and adding the fuel to her nightmares.

Hugging her midsection tightly, she trudged on walking on the sidewalk.

She had no destination when she left, just the feeling of walking and walking to be alone. When her feet began to ache and the drizzle made her clothes feel heavy, she stopped at the local playground and sat under one of the big oak trees.

The sky had darken with the upcoming storm, but Katherine didn't care if she got drenched; she wanted to be alone.

Soon after, it had begun to pour, the raindrops heavy with large splashs in the dirt. Katherine had stayed planted under the tree as it rained, her clothes now soaked and chilling her to the bone.

She found it odd that she was so calm in that moment, after receiving that text message the night before. She didn't lie and say she wasn't terrified; she was scared and paranoid the entire night, which leaked into her dreams. But now, she just felt numb.

Was it because she accepted the reality that she too will die? Be killed by the hands of her sister's murderer? The thought of being with Namie, her only real best friend, gave Katherine a strange sort of comfort.

She had wished for death in these last six years, only Namie's death being the sole trigger, but never had the courage to end it herself. Maybe the man was doing her a favor. She could be realised from this life.

If Namie could see her right now, she'd be begging her to continue living on. She would want Katherine to move on and start living her life in the present instead of the past.

Katherine stood up and wiped away the mud from her pants. Though the road to healing would be a long one, she didn't want to break her promise to Namie. She indeed wanted to be happy, yo continue school and possibly start a family. Who knew when that man would enter her life again, she would need to embrace her remaining days as much as she could.

But sadly, Fate always plans something different with the mere human girl.

As Katherine started to head back home, she heard loud noises coming from behind her. They almost sounded like hooves on the house. But as they appeared, they stopped.

Who could be riding their horse in the rain in a public park?

But that was when she felt the fear crawling up her spine. Dread had latched its fingers around her throat, preventing her from talking.

She knew what this meant; the murderer was behind her.

She could feel him behind her as she stood frozen, unable to move. She knew he was smirking at her helplessness. She prayed that he will deliver her a fast death.

When she braced herself for the pain, she noticed that she felt nothing. She felt no pain or burning in her insides; she was still alive. But why? Was he toying with her, wanting to let her guard down?

Whatever the question may be, she didn't have a chance to know as something hard hit her head, making her collapsed onto the ground unconscious.

He stood above her, his eyes ranking over her small petite frame, her long black hair, and pale olive skin.

"Finally mine, Katherine," he spoke to himself.

But as he went to grab the unconscious girl, he heard horses stomping the dirt and snorting. Turning around, he found a strange man in a dark chariot.

A witness, the deranged man thought. As bad as he wanted to take the girl, he had to leave her and try to hide out as he knew the witness would turn him in. Ditching the girl on the ground, he ran away, never looking back.

The god stepped out of the chariot and bent down to see the girl. She looked uninjured aside from the slight blood trail running down her forehead. He would have his brother heal her before she wakes up.

Being careful not to wake her, he carried her bridal style to the chariot. The horses snorted and huffed, and their master was quick to shush them.

He placed her gently inside the spacious chariot, and with a single wip to the horses, they took off into one of the shadows towards the Underworld.

CHapTer 3

The god sat on his towering throne, sending the souls of the dead into their proper resting places. Most were children and women who had died under brutal deaths, and with the flick of his wrist, their souls were sent to Elysium.

It was truly rare for souls to be sent to Elysium. Most souls tended to be sent to the Asphodel Meadows as their souls were both good and bad, not one side dominating the other.

Elysium was the afterlife for the heroes when the gods had first reigned. It was a place where one's soul could reside in paradise without work for eternity. As the eons came and went, no one would devote themselves to the ancient gods as humans were now inventing technologies, so the god of death decided to have the innocent placed in Elysium.

Most of the innocent souls that were guided to Elysium were of children and women who died of brutal deaths by the hands of man. There was the occasional soul of a man who live his life good without sin, but again, it was rare.

Then there was Tartarus, the deepest region of his kingdom. Souls of the wicked were condemned and sent there to be punished. It was a nine day fall to Tartarus, never knowing when the nine says were up. It was the anticipation that made the souls go made.

As the last round of souls came and went, the god was finally alone in the throne room.

Since Persephone's passing, it was times when all of his duties were completed and he sat on his kingly throne, that he truly felt alone.

The eons of loneliness had taken its toll on the god. Each day, more and more souls came and went and he was aching for her touch. His duties grew and grew, times where even he couldn't finish them all, and having a companion would help significantly.

He had no idea what it was about with the human girl asleep in his chambers that made his frozen heart want to beat. He had remembered her elder sister when she had passed. He had thought that they were identical sisters, but they indeed there was a two year gap between the girls.

Unlike the human girl, her sister was the type that made heads of the opposite sex turn with her curvious frame. But he had felt nothing towards the sister.

He asked her if she remembers how she died, and she told him that she couldn't recall; she couldn't even recall her own family. It was normal for souls to not remember their death. With time, she would come to remember.

That was five years ago. Now, she lives eternity in the fields of Elysium as she awaits for her family.

"Sir," the old man Charos said, his usually quiet voice booming in the large throne room. "All souls have been transported."

"Good," the god spoke, his voice husky. "How is the girl?"

"She is still asleep, but I suspect she will wake shortly."

"Have someone bring her to me when she wakes."

Charos bowed his head at his master. "Sir, if I may ask?" He looked at the fearless god, who motioned for him to continue. "Is the human girl to replace Lady Persephone? You visited her twice my lord, and even brought her to the Underworld--"

Before Charos can finish his sentence, a loud, piercing scream filled the throne room.

The god was quick to stand from his throne and towards his chambers. Chanos stayed behind, watching his masters retreating back.

The old man was curious as to why the lord had an interest in the girl. She was a mere human, she would see her death eventually and arrive here, then the lord could do want he pleased to her soul. But he instead did what he had done with Persephone all those eons ago and took her. Chanos knew that the girl had wished for death since the murder of her sister, and even before that fateful night five years ago. He had heard her prayers and had even considered influencing a human. After all, he was the angel of the dead. But he didn't, as he knew his lord wanted the girl to be alive.

The old man sighed before evaporating into black smoke before he was dragged into the madness.

Katherine had awoken in a fright, having a short lived nightmare. She had dreamt that she was staring over her own dead body, the blood oozing from numerous wounds in her body, her blue foggy eyes staring back at her. Katherine was frozen solid as she continued to stare at her own dead body, and she never realized that there was a man, a very dangerous man behind her, taking joy in her fright. It was she was about to see the man behind her was when she woke up in a daze.

As her mind started to come clearer, she realized that she was not in her room at home. Instead, she was in a massive bedroom chamber. The decor was dark with Gothic archs in the ceiling, elegant black painted walls, and leather furniture that was wore from use. She laid in a massive king sized bed with a canopy above her, it too was black. The covers under her fingers were velvety soft, it was as if she was laying on a cloud.

"Where am I," she asked herself. She got off the bed, with much difficulty, and looked around the chamber. It was truly beautiful, it was as if she was in a Gothic church. It looked like a man's room as the colors were more dark and closed in, but still classy and elegant.

She noticed that she was wearing different clothing from before. Instead of her favorite hoodie and jeans, she now wore a crisp white feminie toga with a gold belt with leaves and flowers craved into the metal. Her hair still felt knotted and tangled. She also was barefoot.

The worse scenarios ran through Katherine's mind: she was kidnapped and was either in her capture's home or a Gothic brothal. Neither sounded pleasent. She looked around for a door too see a massive door in the far corner. She ran to it and yanked on the handle, only for it to be locked. She immediately felt panic course through her as she cried hot tears and opened her mouth and let out a blood cruddling scream.

All of the pent up fears and paranioa had finally broke her as now, she was kidnapped and held hostage. She wondered if she would ever see her parents again. Despite the ways they chose to grieve, Katherine still loved them, and she wished she told them if she knew she would never see them again.

Suddenly, the door opened, knocking her on her butt, to reveal a very handsome man in front of her. He was a tall and muscular figure with broad shoulders and a toned body. He had black hair that went to his ears and curled at the ends and pale skin from not being out in the sun. He wore a black business suit under a black velvet rope. And his eyes... No matter how much Katherine wanted to look away, she couldn't. The man had pitch black eyes, almost soulless, that seemed to glow with an untammed fire, a fire that culd destroy everything in its wake.

"You are awake," he simply said.

Kathrine got up from the floor and stood as far away from the man. Though he was very much attractive, he could very well be the man that killed her sister and kidnapped her. She knew that this man was not to be trusted. Even if he wasn't Namie's killer, he was dangerous. The calm and silent ones are the deadliest.

Katherine didn't bother to answer, not even a simple nod. The man looked irritated by her childish actions, but tried keeping himself calm.

Looking at her this close, the god wondered how this human got to him. She was small for her age and didn't have the body of a mature woman. But wasn't it her childlike looks that drawn him in? Her innocence, her naivity?

"Please, follow me," the god said as he turned around to walk out of his chambers. When he noticed that she hadn't followed him, he grew annoyed and asked her to follow him.

Katherine didn't want to follow the man. For all she knew, he was taking her to a soundproof room to torture her and kill her. But if that was the case, why did he bother and change her out of her wet clothes.

She hesitantly followed him, which the god snuck in a ghost of a smile while she wasn't looking.

Katerine followed her captur into a massive throne like room. A row of white columns on each side of the aisle with several rows of church pews on either side. Up ahead was a platform where a large black throne sat. Katherine marbled at the sight. It was made of black crystals that was chiseled into the form of a throne with gorgeous red rubies in the armrests. She had never seen such a throne made. This man, whoever he was, was obviously wealthy and didn't care for others to marble.

The man went up to the platform and sat at the throne, leaning back in a relax but dominate stature. His aura was powerful, one to keep all eyes on him and him alone. Katherine stood at the bottom of the platform, looking up at the god. She felt smaller as he sat there on the crystal throne.

"Now," the man's voice boomed in the large room. His voice shook Katherine's insides. "I'm sure you're wondering as to where you are and why you're here." Katherine nodded. "Well, I am the Greek god Hades, God of the Underworld. You are here in my palace as I've had a slight interest in you, human. I can't explain it, but you've intrigued me, and as such, I wanted you to come live with me here."

Katherine was silent, her mind reeling. But suddenly, she laughed. She laughed so hard that she had to support herself on her knees. The Greek god was extremely annoyed by her reaction. He had imagined her trying to run in fright from him, not to laugh at his feet like he escaped the pysch ward.

After a few moments, Katherine sobered up and looked up at the extremely irritated god. Her good mood soon disappeared.

The man on the throne abruptly stood up, his dark black eyes shining with an untammed flame, one that turned everything into embers. He had no patience with those who dare mock him. He was a god, a very powerful god. It was obvious that this powerful man did not like those who spoke back or laughed at, espeically by a small human girl like the one in front of him.

The human girl felt the anger radiate off the man and started to run towards the entrance she came from, only to suddenly feel arms wrap around her waist, crushing her against a very solid chest. She opened her mouth to yell, but a strong hand covered her mouth.

"You are a fiesty little girl." It was evident that the man was smirking in his voice; he was enjoying her fear. "Now, I do not want to punish you so early. So please, be the good girl that you are and be quiet. Not that screaming will do you any good; you are in the Underworld, after all. I do not like being made a laughing stock, especially by a mere human like yourself. You will soon see that anyone that pushes my patience will suffer, and trust me; I can make your afterlife miserable. Do you want that, little girl?"

Katherine didn't realize that a mere laugh would make him so angry. At that moment, she did believe that this man was indeed a god, God of the Dead at that. She had read the little mythology they had on the god, and she knew what he was capable of.

She stopped thrishing in his arms, and relucantly, Hades removed his hand from her waist and mouth. "Now was that so hard? Now come, I would like to show you your new home."

Chapter 4

The chariot ride was silent and tense. Katherine sat quietly next to the handsome god, sparing him no glance, paying more attention to the fields of Elysium down below, watching the children play as their mother and father watched with joy. From the descriptions of the Underworld, it was divided into three regoins, Elysium being what Christians believed as heaven, and Tartarus being hell. There were lesser gods in the Underworld that helped run each sector, but Hades was the overall god over the dead.

Soon after, the bright and sunlit fields were replaced with a more typical look with small homes and average looking people. This must be the Asphodel Meadows, where souls who were both good and evil resided. The souls here were human, not perfect. They did wrong, but they also did right. Hades had explained to the human that most souls go to Asphodel Meadows, as the more innocent and heroic went to Elysium.

The Asphodel Meadows soon faded away and as they came across the entrance to Tartarus, Hades commanded the horses to avert from the entrance.

"Was that Tartarus," Katherine asked.

"And the girl speaks," Hades chuckled, trying to lighten the mood. The human rolled her eyes. "But yes, that was the entrance to Tartarus. It is a place you don't want to visit."

"Are the Titans down there?"

"Yes. My father Cronus and many other Titans are down there in sleep by Nyx, Goddess of the night, and her son Hypnos, God of sleep. My mother Rhea is the only Titan that still lives on earth. She takes on human forms and travels from place to place every century. But she does a great job of hiding; no one knows where she resides now."

Katherine nodded, taking in the information. Though she knew little of Greek mythology, she knew that Hades was the brother of Zeus and Poseidon, and were swallowed by Cronus as he feared that they would take his rule over the humans. Zeus had tricked their father into drinking a potion and Cronus threw up Hades and Posideon, along with their sisters Hera, Demeter, and Hestia. That had begun the war between the Gods and the Titans.

Katherine knew that Hades was a private man. He didn't talk about his family, and whenever she would ask a question about them, he either ignored her or changed the topic.

They ended the tour shorty, and soon they landed back at the palace. When landing, Katherine had noticed the beautiful garden below, the flowers bright with vivid colors. She could've sworn that they twinkled and shined like jewels.

"I see you've noticed the garden," Hades asked.

"The flowers are beautiful. May I take a look at them?"

Hades shrugged. "I don't see why not. But I am coming with you; a lost soul sometimes wonders off and they aren't always the friendliest."

Together, they walked down the conjoining staircase from the balcony they landed on.

Katherine's eyes widen as she looked at the flowers. They were in fact twinkling and reflecting lights the artifical sun from above. Taking a closer look, the flowers were made of solid crystals instead of natural petals and stems.

Walking down the small path, the human marveled at the jeweled flowers as the god kept his distance.

It made him slightly proud to see someone seeing his garden. He had orginally made it for Persephone when she missed the world above during her stay. It was a shame that he could not grow natural flowers; he was the god of death. You can't grow things in the land of the dead.

Hades watched the girl become infatuated with one particular flower. It was the first of its own as he created an orignal flower for Persephone. The stem was a dark and shimmering green and the It was in the shape of a rose, but it was a dark blue instead of a traditional red or pink. In the light, it shimmered will many colors, while it turned black like coal in the dark.

"It really is a beautiful flower," she said.

Hades could see that the girl truly liked the jewel. It made the ghost of a smile form on his lips in pride.

Bending over, he was careful to not pluck it too hard as it would shatter, and held it out for Katherine.

The small and sweet gesture from the god shocked Katherine. "You didn't have to do that."

"You obviously marveled it. Take it as my way of apologizing for my behavior earlier. You had caught me in a rather harsh mood."

"You are forgiven." With shaky hands, Katherine went to take the flower from Hades. As she grasped the flower, her fingers lightly brushed against his palm as it sent small shivers up her spine. It was hard to say if the god felt it too, but Katherine merely shook it off and thanked him for the gift.

The day had went by quickly. The artifical sun was beginning to set in the massive cavern. Both she and Hades had spent the day in the graden and had taken a tour of the palace. Katherine knew she would never remember her way around.

Now alone in her seperate chambers, her mind was digesting the fact that she was indeed in the Underworld. At first, she had laughed it off, thinking that Hades has an escapee from the nut house playing make believe. But seeing the different afterlives, the souls, and even the entrance of Tartarus, she now knew that it was reality.

She began to wonder if her parents had even noticed that she was gone. Probably not though. Dean and Rachelle Bakers had stopped caring about their own daughter after Namie's death, stuck in their own grief.

Wait, was Namie here in the Underworld? If she was, was she in Elysium or in the Asphodel Meadows? Was she happy in her afterlife?

"Why don't you just ask yourself?"

Katherine snapped out of her thoughts at the very familiar voice, a voice she hadn't heard in five long years. Looking up, she saw her sister standing in the doorway, a bright smile etched into her face.

CHAPTER 5

In an instant, Katherine jumped off the bed and ran to her sister, unshed tears blinding her. She crashed into Namie and they both fell to the floor, grunts turning into laughter.

Five years. Five long years since they've seen each other; one being a soul in Elysium, the other having to face her own hell back home.

"I can't believe you're here," Katherine cried. "Am I dreaming? Is this another cruel nightmare?"

"Not this time Kat," Namie cooed. A wave of fresh tears overcame Katherine at the sound of her nickname. Only Namie called her Kat.

Getting up off the floor, the younger sister continued to stare at the soul of her sister. She looked exactly the same; choppy black hair and olive skin. But she wore the same type of toga Katherine had, and her body would shimmer in transparency. She did not float like the stereotypical ghosts; she looked human.

Namie too stared at her sister. She noticed that Katherine dud not change much since she was fourteen, aside from her long hair. Her frame was small and petite like a child's and Namie could've sworn she looked thinner the longer she looked.

"God, I've missed you so much, Namie. How are you here? Aren't you suppose to be in Elysium?"

Namie chuckled. "I was for a while as I couldn't remember much about my life when I was alive. I didn't remember you, mom and dad, my death, anything. Hades had placed me in Elysium hoping I would regain my memory.

"My memories came back in fragments. I would see something that reminded me of when I was alive and try to piece the puzzle. Luckily, my memory came back soon after, and since then I have been worried sick about you."

"I did hear some of your rambling when you would visit my grave."

Katherine blushed in embarrassment. Most of the time, she pretended that Namie was standing in front of her, not dead, and have a quiet conversation, ranging from life back home to nostalgic memories.

She didn't think Namie heard everything.

"So, why aren't you in your afterlife?"

"Lord Hades came and visited me and told me that you were in the Underworld. Immediately I thought you were dead, but he assured me that you were very much alive. He knew that we were close and asked me to be your 'personal escort' while you're here. He never told me why you were here in the first place; just that you were in trouble and brought you here to keep you safe."

Katherine nodded. She told Namie about almost bring attacked at the park by her murderer. She was surprised that he didn't kill her, but instead knocked her out. After that, she couldn't remember, and she awoke in Hades chambers.

"And so here I am. I'm not going to lie that Hades scares me; he terrifies me. I'm afraid that if I say something wrong, he'll do something."

Namie too worried about this. Like her sister, she knew little about the myths surrounding the god. The few that were documented described Hades as a ruthless god who ruled with an iron fist and cruel punishments. The famous myth being about Persephone.

Persephone was the Goddess of spring, and was the daughter to Demeter and Zeus. One day, while in a field, the earth opened up and came Hades in his dark chariot. He grabbed the girl and took her to the Underworld to be his wife. Demeter was so furious, she put the earth under a harsh winter, killing the harvest and even humans.

Zeus told Hades to return Persephone, but by then, she had eaten the seeds of a pomegranate and could not leave as eating from the land of the dead trapped a person. Zeus bargained with Hades to allow Persephone to spend half the year with her mother and the other half with him.

Each version of the tale is different. One saying Hades kidnapped her; another saying it was an arranged marriage. One said she was forced to eat the seeds; another said she willingly ate them so she could be with Hades.

Whatever might be the true myth, it was the same.

Was Hades planning to make Katherine his queen? To be Persephone's replacement?

Namie chose to not to speak her thoughts aloud. It would only add to the fear Katherine still held for the god.

Katherine noticed her sister's change in mood, but decided to not ask her. She was still floating in the clouds after seeing her sister. No words of gratitude were enough at Hades effort to make Katherine enjoy her stay.

The two sisters laughed and talked for what seemed like hours. As Namie was her 'personal escort,' she would attend all of her sister's needs from clothes to hygienics.

It still felt weird to see Namie as an escort. She was still seeing her as her sister, her best friend. It would be weird at first, but Katherine would get use to it.

It was late that night that Namie had to go. Katherine was reluctant to say goodbye to her sister. She was afraid that this was all a dream, and she would wake back up in her own room.

Namie noticed this, and reassured her that she would be back in the morning.

Katherine reluctantly said goodnight to Namie, and with a brief hug, Namie exited her room.

Namie sighed as she closed the massive wooden doors, the dark cravings rough under her skin. The cravings showed a picture of the earth with lushous green meadows and flowers, while below was a deep cavern, the edges sharp and jagged.

"What do you plan to do with my sister," the girl asked the god behind her.

Hades chuckled, surprised that she sensed him behind her. "Why do you want to know?"

"Because I don't want her to be forced into marriage with you like Perseph–"

Before she could finish, strong hands wrapped around her throat, squeezing.

The god's eyes were bright with anger. "I will not tolerate this in my own home. Katherine will have a choice if the time comes. She is interest for me. You mortals think that I am a monster, capable of kidnapping and forcing myself on the weak. Speak one word to Katherine, and I will throw you into Tartarus so fast it'll make your head spin. Do not test me, spirit."

The god let go of the girl, and she fell to the floor, gasping.

"I'm only looking our of my sister. She is the only family I have here. Take me away, and she will hate and despise you."

"That is why you will keep quiet. She has simply caught my interest and curiousity, nothing more. So far." He whispered the last part to himself.

He turned and walked away from the girl, feeling the icy glare she threw at him.

CHAPTER 6

A week has passed since Katherine arrived in the Underworld. To her, that week was stretched into years, each second feeling like hours.

Despite having Namie around, Katherine still felt alone. Namie was only with her for a few hours in the day as she had other things to attend to in the palace, and with the god busy with the dead, Katherine longed for company.

She spent most of her time in her room; and if she wasn't in her room, she was in the garden or in the library. She would spend hours reading books of the different legends on the original gods or staring at the jeweled flowers.

Katherine began to think that this life was no different than the life she had before. Even the hole she thought Namie could fill was still there in her heart. She wondered why she still felt alone when she was with her sister.

The artificial sun glared down at the human girl, the cavern still dark with jagged rocks in the ceiling. Today, she was in the garden, sitting on a small bench near the center of the garden.

The little bit of the garden she saw her day with Hades was nothing compared to the rest. In the center was a small hedge maze with green walls reaching forever into the cavern ceiling. In the center of the maze was a magnificent coble fountain with a beautiful sculpture of a young nymph. She looked so real on the pedestal, her hair like a waterfall down her shoulders and her dress flowy. Katherine often envied the statures beauty.

Every once in a while, a spirit or a nymph would pass by through the maze. They looked at her and smiled, confused as to why their lord brought a human to the Underworld.

The solitude brought some sort of peace to Katherine. Though she was often lonely, being alone brought more peace than loneliness, despite bring alone for most of her teenage years.

Katherine laid down on the bench, staring up at the cavern ceiling. She began to think what her parents are up to. No doubt they hadn't noticed her absence; her father in the office and her mother in another man's bed.

Katherine loved her parents, even though she knew they had abandoned her in grief. They didn't see their only daughter, even when Namie was alive. No right person would love parents like that; but Katherine did.

"Enjoying the view," a voice said, breaking her thoughts.

Katherine immediately sat up, having been scared of the god in front of her. He chest vibrated with his chuckles and the corners of his eyes crinkled as he smiled. Katherine noticed he looked more handsome–if it was even possible–as he smiled.

Today, he wore a classic black suit instead of the velvet rope he traditionally wore, his tone muscles and broad shoulders snug in the suit. His black hair was combed back, and his black eyes seemed to burn with smothered embers.

Katherine still thought of Hades as a very dangerous man, but the devil was always beautiful as he was God's favorite.

Hades noticed that the girl was staring at him, but didn't tell. He knew she would be embarrassed to be staring, but a part of him didn't mind. Something always seemed to stir inside of him when Katherine got the chance to look from the thick veil known as her hair. It made his stomach feel warm.

But he always pushed those feelings away. Even if he was infatuated with the girl, she would never have him. He was a god, the god of death. His darkness would taint her.

But he promised to give it a shot. It's not like he had much longer anyways.

"You scared me half to death," Katherine said to Hades once her speeding heart calmed down. Hades chuckled at her unintended pun. "I didn't expect to see you hear."

"I didn't have much work today, and thought to accompany you, if you didn't mind."

"No, of course. How did you know I was here?"

He shrugged. "Lucky guess."

Katherine shook her head, stood up from her bench, and vegan to walk back out the maze. When she noticed Hades hadn't followed, she turned her shoulder and raised an eye-brow. "You coming?"

Hades and Katherine walked the massive garden together, making various small talks. Katherine felt at ease when Hades talked to her. She had thought it was due to her lack of attention over the years, and didn't dwell on it.

"You know," Katherine thought aloud. "I don't think I've ever seen Cerberus around. Where is he?"

"Do you want to see him?"

"Really? Is it safe?"

Hades smiled. "He is completely friendly, so I don't see the harm. Though, he is not what you humans picture him to be."

Not like he seems?

Katherine followed Hades to the back edge of the garden. In the shade of trees there was several small dog houses, each different but extravagant in designs. Why were they heading towards a few dog kettles?

Hades stopped at one particular. This one was larger than the others, this one like a replica of the palace.

He clicked his tongue against his teeth and softly spoke in his native tongue. Katherine heard a loud howl like a yawn coming from the house, and after a few moments, a small dog with three heads came out from the house.

The small dog had three separate heads, each with its own personality: the left one looking half asleep, the center one yapping in delight, and the right one with a slight frown in his muzzle. It had a very shiny black coat that glistened in the sun.

"Come here, Cerberus."

Cerberus' three heads snapped their heads at their owner and eagerly ran up to him.

"That's Cerberus?" Katherine asked when Hades picked up the gate keeper of the Underworld.

"I told you you humans painted another picture of Cerberus. Always making death dramatic."

To say Katherine was shocked was an understatement. She had always pictured Cerberus to be a giant beast who helped protect the Underworld and guard the gates to the entrance.

"Would you like to hold him?"

"Are you sure?"

"He is completely harmless."

Hades spoke to the dog, telling it about his 'new friend' and to not harm her. Hades knew the dog understood. He gently placed Cerberus in Katherine's arms, and immediately, the dog took a liking to the girl, licking her face.

Katherine laughed as the tiny dog lick her. She didn't notice that the god beside her was admiring her.

CHapTer 7

The next few weeks came and went in a blur, and before too long, it was Halloween.

Growing up, the sisters loved Halloween. It was the only time they dressed up as gruesome creatures to scare others. When they were smaller, they had a competition to see which one could get the most candy. Of course, Katherine always won.

Katherine awoke in the morning of Halloween, a big smile already stretching her face. It was her first Halloween there in the Underworld, and she wondered how Hades did Halloween here.

Getting up from her massive bed, she wrapped herself in her silk robe and walked out into the hall.

The dark hall was decorated with purple lights, leaves, pumpkins, and spiderwebs. Maids and servants worked furiously to get the palace decorated for tonight.

The night before, Hades explained to Katherine that the gods host a massive ball on Halloween night called the Hallows Eve Ball. Everyone wears costumes or any outfit they choose. He recited times when his niece, Aphrodite would wear the shortest and skimpest costumes known to man, or Dionysus getting insanely hammered and making trouble.

The way Hades told of his family was like they were like any normal crazy family; not gods that saw over the earth since creation. She also had no idea about the minor gods and creatures that guided and helped humans. For example, Aphrodite's son Eros, the god love and desire. They all branched off in different directions, but they all came from the original.

Katherine made her way to the throne room. She knew Hades would be there, as he normally was. She use to think that he slept in that marble throne.

The throne room was still as grand as her first day three weeks ago. The pews for the souls were gone, leaving the area open for the ball tonight. Cobwebs hung in every corner and candles floating in the air, casting dark shadows across the room.

The throne sat on the platform, and she still felt intimidated by the massive size of it. It's black marble shape caught the light from the candles and it shimmered and glittered.

But what caught her eye was a more smaller throne next to the larger one. Unlike it's counterpart, this throne was pure white with pearls in the armrests and other pale jewels.

Why did Hades add another throne? Was it his wife's?

Come to think about it, Katherine has yet to see his wife; Persephone, the daughter of Demeter. It was one of the most recognizable myths of Hades. Hades never mentioned

Persephone to the human, nor engaged in any talks about her. The servants would whisper among themselves about their master. When Katherine would ask them, they denied anything and continued back to work.

Curiosity crept up on Katherine. A small part of her wanted to sit on the throne. She wanted to see it from Hades' eyes.

Looking around to see if anyone was around, she walked up the stairs and onto the platform. The thrones up close were both intimidating yet beautiful. Hades' throne up close, she noticed the different shards of jewels embedded into the marble, and the white one looked to be made of diamond.

Doubling checking to see if anyone saw her, she cautiously walked up to the smaller throne and sat down.

It was surprisingly comfortable despite it being made of diamond. She felt tall as she looked at the room below her. She imagined the pews of souls, waiting for the final resting place. She imagined Hades sitting in his throne and her next to him, guiding souls and providing comfort to those who were hesitate.

Wait, she thought. Why I am thinking like this? This is nuts. Already three weeks in and I'm already thinking like this.

"This throne does suite you," a smooth and monotone said behind Katherine.

Katherine jumped up from the throne, but it was pointless; Hades knew that she snuck onto the platform.

The god was hiding in the shadows, wearing his helmet so the human wouldn't see her. He watched her as she sat there. In some ways, she reminded him of Persephone. Despite the physical difference, they were both shy and had new found awe in the Underworld, seeing beauty in death.

Their first day in the garden made him see that. Katherine was tranced by the jeweled flowers, and Cerberus immediately took a liking to her. It was nearly impossible to take Cerberus from her arms as the pup whined and howled. The nymphs even spoke fondly of the girl, praising her for admiring their work.

Everything felt brighter with Katherine. Lighter even. Everyone was worried for Hades after Persephone's passing. But seeing this new girl brought hope. Hades hoped that this girl can save him.

The human's cheeks flushed red, being caught at the queen's throne. Hades bit the inside of his cheek to keep himself from chuckling.

He was telling the truth; the throne did suite her.

"I-I'm so sorry," the mortal stuttered.

"It's alright," Hades smiled. "I had it brought up for you. You are my guest, and I want you to be comfortable at the ball."

Katherine wanted to ask if it was Persephone's throne, but decided against it.

"Oh! You didn't have to; I didn't want to burden you with that."

"Don't worry your head with it. Speaking of the ball, are you planning on a dress or costume?"

"Dress. I'm not telling you what it is though."

Hades was almost shocked at the flirtiness from the human. Katherine didn't catch it, and Hades didn't mention it. It was cute.

"If you must keep the suspense, then so be it."

Katherine giggled.

She was too embarrassed about the dress. When picking it out, Namie assured her that it was lovely and that it suited the theme.

All too soon, Katherine was ushered by Namie and another maid to her chamber to get ready. Though the ball wasn't until later on in the night, Katherine had to get in a corset, which she was dreading.

When they got to her chamber, Katherine was shoved into a chair and Namie worked on her hair and makeup as the second maid prepared the dress.

Namie worked a brush through her sister's thick black hair. She saw Kat wince, but she pulled through. Namie was skilled in cosmetology. The older sister twisted the hair and began to pin it to her head. Since the dress and makeup would be the eye catchers, the hair would be simple.

After a few minutes, Namie pinned the elegant sock bun and added a few dark red roses to the look. A few curls were left framing Katherine's face.

Katherine didn't have time to marble at her hair, before Namie spun her around away from the mirror to do her makeup.

"I want it to be a surprise," Namie said as Katherine made a face. "Don't make that look."

For the next hour, Namie painted Katherine's face. She applied light foundations on her sister's face, then applied a red smokey eye to the eyelids to match the dress. When Namie was about to apply the black eyeliner, Katherine outright refused it. But after assuring her, Namie continued, careful to not poke her sister's eye.

Finally, after the finishing touches, Namie was done with the makeup. She couldn't help but beam at her work. Despite being wary of any of Hades' intentions for her little sister, Namie hoped that Katherine had gun tonight.

"Can I look now?" Katherine whined.

Namie smirked. "Not yet."

The maid from before, Katherine learned her name was Cattie, quickly got the dress from the bed and held it up.

The dress was an elegant gown with ruffles on the skirt and a tight corset bodest. It was black with a bright crimson red that matched the dark theme of the ball. Though it didn't have traditional sleeves, it came with a small lace top that button in the front.

Katherine quickly undressed, making sure to not ruin the makeup and hair and put on the tights for the dress.

It took several minutes to get the dress on. The corset felt constricting and Katherine was having trouble breathing properly. The lace top felt itchy because it was such a foreign texture against her skin. She felt like a Western prostitute.

Slipping on the matching red heels, Katherine was ready. Butterflies buzzed in her stomach, making her feel ill. She swallowed the bile at the back of her throat.

As if sensing her nerves, Namie reassured her. "Don't be nervous. You look grand."

All Katherine could do was nod and smile.

"Milady," Cattie called out. "Lord Hades is here to escort you."

"Let him in."

Katherine's hands began to sweat. She was worried that Hades would not like the dress. It did embrace her chest, an area she didn't lack. And it made her waist tiny as a Barbie's.

The chamber doors opened and the god himself stepped through.

He was a loose white shirt with the first two buttons undone and tight leather pants low on his hips, with a long cape clasped together by a single gold chain. He wore a mask that resembled one that the Phantom of the Opera, his hair slicked and flipped off to the side, highlighting his cheek bones.

"Where's Katherine?"

"Through here," the maid said, slightly intimidated.

Hades followed the maid around the corner and in the middle stood the tiny human girl.

He had to check to see if his jaw was opened.

The tight corset bodest showed off her curves and chest, despite the attempts of the lace top. The red eyeshadow made her eyes pop as did the red lipstick. Her long black hair was tied into an elegant bun with small roses and tiny pieces of hair framing her round face perfectly.

The god sworn that his heart began to beat, even if it was for a fraction of a second.

"Hades," Namie said sturdily at the god, seeing how his graze was towards her sister.

Hades snapped his attention from Katherine to Namie, his intense gaze reminding her of their conversation. She couldn't stop him. If he had interest in the girl, he would explore it.

Katherine was oblivious to the tension between the two.

"You look beautiful, Katherine," Hades said. He wasn't lying.

He saw Katherine blushed, and he but his tongue to stop from chuckling at her oblivious cuteness.

"Are you ready?"

"Not that I have a choice in the matter," Katherine joked.

She took his extended hand, intertwining her arm around his. She felt the coldness from him, but it felt comfortable and calming to her. The skin through the lace felt like it was on fire from touching him.

What was he doing to her?

Hades hid the smile well, not wanting her to see that he too, was having the same affect as well.

They walked through the decorated halls in silence. Katherine was afraid to talk. She was about to meet Hades family, the Gods of Olympus. To say she was intimidated would be an understatement.

They reached a set of closed doors that lead to the throne room. Katherine's hands became clammy and her knees slightly buckled. The butterflies were violent in her stomach.

"Relax," Hades cooed. "They'll respect you as you're a guest here under my protection."

Katherine nods, his words sinking in. She took a few breaths—it was still difficult with the corset—and forced herself to calm down.

Two maids that stood on either side of the entrance opened the doors, the light serving through the growing gap.

Whatever Katherine was expecting as a ball with the gods, was definitely not what the reality in front of her.

CHAPTER 8

The throne room was packed with men and women, all wearing either formal wear or costumes. The candles casted long shadows on the floor and walls and the cobwebs and jack-o-lanterns made the room feel dark and old, a spooky type of vibe.

The large hall was packed with men and women in formal wear or costumes. Couples danced in the center, dancing to the harmony of the music as spectators watched and talked of gossip. It was hard to tell who were the gods and goddesses, Hades family, but the haunting mood of the ball had pushed away the anxiety.

Katherine stared in awe at the sight. Her nerves were gone, replaced with adrenaline and excitement. A smile was permanently etched into her face.

Hades had to steal another glance at her. She looked beautiful when she smiled, which was rare. While preparing Namie for her new role, she had told him times that Katherine was jealous of her, as Namie was the favorite among their parents. Namie knew, even if Katherine hid it well. She told him that she suffered depression through most of their lives, and developed self-destructive habits.

A large part of him admired Katherine for staying strong. He could only imagine the dark thoughts that would run through her head, the death of her sister only triggering more of those thoughts.

He subconsciously shook his head. He was a cold hearted god, since when did he admire humans?

Since Katherine showed up.

They walked together the center of the room, eyes naturally being drawn to the couple. Katherine felt eyes on her, and her hands began to sweat again. She didn't like having attention on her.

"Don't worry about them," Hades cooed quietly in her ear. "Pretend that no one is here."

Easier said than done, Katherine thought bitterly.

The crowd broke apart to let them onto the dance floor. Those who were dancing stepped onto the side to let the god and human dance.

Hades removed her arm from his and stood in front of her. He bowed, gesturing his hand towards her, silently asking her for a dance. Katherine curtsy and gently placed her hand in his, accepting his invitation. Hades straightened up and pulled her body close to his, one hand on her waist and the other still holding her hand. Katherine placed her hand on his shoulder, feeling the taunt muscles flex underneath her touch.

The music began. Hades started it slow, only making small steps in a small circle. The nerves from feeling eyes on her were back and butterflies buzzed in the pit of her stomach.

"Pretend that no one is there."

Katherine took a deep breath, calming her nerves. She loosened her tight grip on his hand, and let the music overtake her.

Hades noticed her sudden calmness, and now, he freely danced with her, twirling her and moving at a faster pace.

Katherine's body hummed as she and the god danced. Her body was like liquid, flowing along with the music. She didn't tell Hades that she use to take ballroom dancing when she was little.

It seemed like eternity as they danced. The nerves was completely gone and Katherine no longer noticed the eyes of the patrons. She was lost in the music as she danced with Hades, never breaking eye contact.

The longer she stared at Hades, the more she noticed small details. Like the faint scar that cut into the corner of his lips, tiny dots of freckles on his nose, or how much his black eyes swirled. Black eyes were meant to be cold and bitter, but his were soft and burned with an untamed flame.

When she first met him, he was frightening, treating her with punishment. But over the previous weeks, in moments like this, she saw this side, a side that he didn't let others see. If anyone saw this side, they would see him as weak and try to take over his kingdom.

All too soon, the song ended and the dance ended. Both of them bowed, silently thanking each other for the dance.

The silent hall erupted into clapping and cheers. Heat rose to Katherine's cheeks as Hades pulled her away from the dance floor.

"I didn't realize you could dance," Hades said, his voice evident of the pride he felt.

"I took ballroom lessons growing up. It was one thing I truly enjoyed, and one thing I was actually good at."

"That couldn't be the only thing."

"It was. I didn't have friends besides Namie. I was the loner in the back that no one noticed. In a lot of ways, I preferred it that way."

Hades related to Katherine. Like her, he preferred to the solitude that the Underworld provided. Even though he had family, he couldn't stand more than a few hours with them. Katherine was in her sister's shadow, her parents only seeing Namie. His cold heart went out to her.

They stayed side by side for another hour. Katherine drunk a few glasses of strawberry champagne and snacks. At one point, Katherine took off her heels, the blisters irritating her.

Hades had to attend to something, leaving Katherine alone. Some glanced at her, either admiring her for her dancing or glaring her down, despite her sitting on the throne Hades provided her. She would've sunk down if not for the tight corset.

After a little while, when Hades hadn't return, Katherine ventured out back to the main floor. The cool floor sent small shivers up her spine.

She stood at the edges of the crowd, watching others enjoy themselves. She still hadn't seen any of Hades' family. It was hard to tell who was who in the sea of masks.

"You must be the human my brother took in," a husky voice said beside her.

Her heart jumped at the surprise. She hadn't realized someone stood beside her.

She looked at the side and saw a very handsome man, towering over her. He had similar features as Hades: strong jawline, high chiseled cheekbones, and a muscular body with broad shoulders and muscles that looked stretched in his too tight skin. But he had tan skin and blonde hair. His chest was bare, his abs chiseled, and he wore white cloth about his hips.

There was something about him that seemed off. Katherine couldn't put her finger on it. Maybe it was the champagne talking to her.

"Sorry, I haven't introduced myself. I am Apollo. I am assuming you know what I do, human?"

"You're the God of music, medicine, archery, and the sun. And your sister is Artemis."

Apollo smiled fondly at the girl. "Impressive. I didn't take you as one to now my family."

"I spend a lot of time in the library."

Hades stared intensely at Katherine and his nephew Apollo. Something foreign stirred in his stomach. He didn't like the fact that Apollo has already taken a liking to her, and seeing how the other men practical drooled over her made him tremble. He knew Apollo was serious trouble, he had hoped he wouldn't show. His hand subconsciously tightened around the glass he held, almost breaking it.

"Jealous aren't we brother," Zeus asked with a smirk. "By the way you are staring at your nephew, I would say you have feelings for the human."

"Don't kid yourself," Poseidon laughed. "No one can get his icy heart thawed. Not since her."

"True as it may be, I don't have feelings for Katherine," Hades said through gritted teeth.

"You don't have long, brother," Zeus said, his playful tone gone. "You have to have a Queen. You don't have long."

"I still have a few years left."

"Still, dont wait. I know that since her, you've felt bleak and miserable. But you need to let go and find someone. Though we always argue, we do not want to see our brother fade out of existence."

Hades was silent. Zeus spoke the truth. Without Persephone, he believed his life was meaningless. But since seeing Katherine, something had risen up from the darkness. Around her, his heart began to beat; he felt relaxed when she smiled; she felt right when they danced.

Could she really be the one?

CHAPTER 9

The ball was still in full swing. People continued to dance and drink. After talking with Apollo, Katherine met the other gods and goddesses. They didn't mind that she was barefoot and drunk, half of them were drunk as well.

She had met Hades' brothers Zeus and Poseidon. Zeus was muscular with bronzed skin and golden blonde hair. His skin seemed to glitter. He wore a simple black suit with a mask. Posideon was slightly shorter than his brother, with long brown hair tied into a low ponytail and deeply tanned skin. In his hand, he held a golden trident, the instrument glittering in the candlelight.

After speaking with them, she moved on to meet Dionysus, though he mostly drank and made crude jokes than talk. She didn't get the chance to meet Ares or Hephaestus, but she didn't mind.

None of the goddesses were present, which seemed weird to Katherine, but she was too drunk to care.

Around twelve in the morning, Katherine called it a night. Her mind was foggy from the alcohol and her body ached from the hours in a corset. When she couldn't find Hades to tell him goodnight, she stumbled out of the throne room, the hall deathly quiet versus the noise from the ball.

She stumbled into a chair, groaning as her head spun. The walls tilted and spun, the floor seeming to disappear and reappear under her feet.

Why had she drunk so much? She was light with alcohol, she wasn't Dionysus.

"Can't the human hold her liquor?"

Katherine looked to see Apollo standing behind her, very close to her. When did he get there? And why was he standing so close to her?

Now that they were alone in the hall, Katherine felt a little uneasy. His eyes trailed down her body, lingering on her tiny waist and chest, making her squirm.

Back home, she wasn't much to look at. Sure, boys drooled over her chest and butt, but she hid in a hoodie. Whenever Hades would look at her, she felt warm inside and kinda giddy, like a school girl crush.

But Apollo...why did she feel weird and uncomfortable with him? And why couldn't the knot in her stomach go away?

When Apollo reached for her, she held up a hand, gripping the arm of the chair.

"Please, I'm fine. Don't let me take you away from the ball."

"I don't mind," he smiled. "I much rather have your company."

Katherine bit back a groan. She didn't say anything when Apollo grabbed her waist and guided her to her room. His fingers dug into her waist, his fingers itching against the corset. She could practically feel his eyes trying to peak a glance at her chest.

The made it to her room. Katherine tried to pull away, but Apollo kept his grip tight. She whimpered and tried to push him off her, but he was solid as a rock.

"G-Get off me," she slurred.

"Why? Don't you like it? Does Hades hold you like this?"

Hades?

"Hades..."

"I bet he hasn't touched you, not even a hug," Apollo smiled smugly. "He'll never get over Persephone. She had his heart in her hands. He would do anything. He won't even hug you. I can do anything you want me to. I can give you more than he can."

Apollo dipped his head into the crook of her neck, kissing the sensitive skin. Even in her drunken state, Katherine knew she didn't want this.

She tried pushing and shoving at him, but he kept his grip tight. At one point, Apollo opened the door to her room and pushed her through, closing the door behind them.

Katherine's eyes widen in fear. She was all alone. Hades didn't know where she was and Namie wouldn't be back till the morning.

She saw the lust thick in Apollo's eyes, the bulge in his pants a dead giveaway. She tried putting distance between them, but her dress got caught under her feet, causing her to fall.

Before she could get up, Apollo climbed on top of her, straddling her hips. His hands grabbed her wrists and pinned them above her head.

"Why are you fighting? You know you want to be touched. Hades obviously won't give it to you. Let me..."

Using his free hand, the god ripped off the skirt of the dress, leaving the human in a corset. The cool air sent goosebumps up her spine. He tore at the corset, tearing it to shreds. Katherine now laid in her bra and underwear.

Silent tears streamed down her face. "Please, d-don't this ..."

Apoll smiled. It was unfriendly. "Don't worry, you'll enjoy this."

Katherine cried as the sound of a camera snapping rung in the air. She felt sore in between her legs, her arms feeling limped. She felt too weak to fight.

"Don't cry baby," Apollo cooed. "Just a few more."

He was finally gone. Apollo left when the ball was over. When asked, Katherine would say that he stayed with her while she slept to watch over her.

He also made sure to keep her silent. He didn't want his reputation ruined, specially by a mere human.

Katherine laid on the floor with her tattered dress. Her tears were dry, and her body was slowly gaining strength. She knew Namie would be arriving soon.

Pushing herself off the floor, Katherine gathered her ru-ined dress and hid it in the back of the closet. She hurried to the bathroom. She felt dirty and used, his touch still lingering. Her body was covered in bites and scratches on areas where no one would see them.

Turning on the tap, she stepped under the water and tried to wash away his touch. No matter how hard she scrubbed, she still felt dirty. Even after she was red and raw.

Getting out of the shower, she dried herself off, avoiding her reflection.

No one would believe her. Apollo was a hod, she a human. They would take the word of their own over a human girl. She couldn't tell anyone, not even Hades or Namie.

She got dresses in jeans and a baggy sweater and walked out of the bathroom. As expected, Namie was there. Katherine plastered on a fake smile.

"Hey sis. How was the ball?"

Katherine shrugged. "It was fun. Hades and me danced; he didn't know I took ballroom. He was very surprised."

"I've been wondering about that. A lot of servants have been talking about hey our dance. 'Very intimate' they say."

The word intimate made something stir in her stomach, and not in a good way?

What would Hades think if he found out? Would he see her as useless, as trash? Would he believe his nephew over her? Would he ever believe her?

She couldn't tell him. She couldn't tell him that she was raped by Apollo.

CHAPTER 10

It wasn't hard for Katherine to avoid Hades, she rarely saw him during the day. She never went to the throne room while souls were in there.

Her hangover and the wounds from the night before were still very fresh, so she went to the library seeking solitude from everything. She didn't want to see her nymph company or her sister.

Earlier that morning, Katherine tried to keep the conversation from the ball. Namie was curious on what happened, did she and Hades do anything or did she meet someone. Instead of answering, she stirred the question away.

Namie could sense that something was wrong. She could read Katherine like a book. She knew something happened at the ball, something bad. Namie would notice how Kat would fidget if she stared too long and she didn't eat anything.

After Katherine left for the library, Namie headed straight to the throne room. She may not know what happened, but something in her mind Hades had to something with it. He was a god after all, he had no boundaries.

Throwing open the doors, Namie walked down the long aisle, ignoring the curious stares from the souls.

"Lord Hades," Namie said sternly.

The god on the throne looked up from the tablet he held, his eyes holding annoyance. He didn't like being interrupted during his work.

Though the god would never say it aloud, he was mad at Katherine. He had tried to find her at the ball but couldn't find her. The only thought was that she went to someone's bed. The thought of that made him furious. She didn't even tell him goodnight or where she was heading. He was worried, but worried as replaced by anger.

"What is it?" The god asked, already bored.

"We need to talk," Namie looked at the souls, "privately."

"You can say it here."

"It's about..."

She didn't even have to finish the sentence; Hades knew she meant Katherine. He quickly stood from the throne, told the souls to wait a few moments, and followed Namie into the hall.

"What's wrong–"

"What did you do yo my sister?!" Namie yelled.

Hades' eyes glowed violently. "What do you mean?"

"I know you did something to Kat. She was completely different from last night, and you were the last person she was with!"

The last person...?

"You promised that you wouldn't take advantage of her!"

"Namie–"

"You god's are all the same; just take, take, take."

"Namie–"

"Why did you even hurt–"

"NAMIE!"

Namie quickly shut her mouth, glaring at Hades.

"What is wrong with Katherine?"

"She kept fidgeting if I stared at her for too long, avoided any talk of the ball, and didn't eat anything this morning. She may hide it, but I know somethings wrong. I assumed you did something."

"Katherine, I have not touched your sister. After our dance was the last time I saw her. She talked to some of my family. They could know something."

"Who did she talk to?"

"My brothers Zeus and Posideon, Eros, Dionysus, and... Apollo." He spat out Apollo's name like it was poison.

"You don't think they did something to her, do you?"

"Despite myths, the gods are rarely with humans, only when we see fit to create heroes. The only one would be..."

The worst of the worse came to Hades' mind. Did Apollo...

"I'm worried for her," Namie whispered. "She hasn't had a depressive episode since she was thirteen. She had the same look as before; lost and broken. She'll want to do things to help the pain. I can't watch her go through that..."

Hades could see the love and struggle in Namie's eyes. She truly did love her sister. She was the one that told her it was going to be okay, to keep being strong. Now with the thought that someone hurt Katherine made Namie weep.

Hades didn't tell her about his suspension, it would only make it worse. Without Katherine to testify, it was going to be hard to know if Apollo did something. Hades had to be careful about his investigation; one wrong move and Apollo would know and possibly harm Katherine thinking she told. He needed evidence. What evidence isn't hidden somewhere in Apollo's home.

"Where is she?"

"Library."

Hades quickly sent a message to Charos to stop passage to the Underworld till he gave orders to resume. He walked quickly to the library, the pit in his stomach growing.

He cared for the human. He hid it well, but he cared. She had an innocence about her that couldn't be tainted by the constant darkness around her. If she lost that innocence, she would be a shell of her former self.

He hoped that his suspensions were wrong. He truly did.

Growing up, Katherine loved to read. She had piles of books on her desk, self, and beside her bed on the floor. After Namie's death, Katherine would read yo escape her life. She would read for hours and hours, never stopping. If she stopped, only bad thoughts would come.

She sat in the far corner of the second floor in the library. There was a large fireplace with a roaring fire and a comfortable couch to sit on.

In her hands was an old Spanish story translated into English. Though she didn't care for historical fiction, she enjoyed the book. And despite starting the large book a few hours ago, Katherine had a chunk of it read.

She was so entranced by the story, she didn't notice Hades standing above her. He stood silently, watching her read, her eyebrows furrowed close in concentration.

When she finally noticed him, she flushed with embarrassment, realizing that she practically ignored him.

"Sorry. I didn't see you there."

Hades forced a chuckle. "It's alright. Mind if I sit with you?"

She shook her head and moved her feet to leave a space for Hades. He sat down, a decent distance between them, even if it was a small couch. They say in silence, Katherine watching the fire crack and Hades watching her.

Katherine knew he was looking at her, and it made her skin crawl. A lump formed in her throat, and she tried to swallow it down. Her body shifted ever so slightly, moving away from the god. Any human wouldn't have noticed, but Hades did.

His face was blank, but in his mind, that small movement confirmed his fears. He knew he had to wait till he had evidence before asking her.

"How did you enjoy the ball?" Hades asked, the thick silence broken.

"It was good. I had a bit too much champagne."

"That was Dionysus' courtesy. He always liked harder liquor."

"I'm a natural light weight. It wouldn't have mattered."

So she was drunk when...

"How come none of the goddesses were at the ball?"

"They were, but they like to keep hidden, especially Aphrodite. She loves a game of cat and mouse with Hephaestus. The others like to hide as a way to be 'normal.' Even the Gods and Goddesses of Olympus need a break."

"Makes sense."

They fell back into silence, the air thick between them. Katherine subconsciously had her arms around her, hugging herself. Hades wanted to blurt it out, that he knew Apollo hurt her. He wanted her to confirm his fears.

"Did any of my family treat you well?"

"Zeus and Posideon was nice, Eros was focused on getting laid, Dionysus was drunk, and... Apollo seemed nice..." Her body stiffened at his name.

Memories of last night were fresh in her mind. She tried to block it out.

"What happened to you last night? I couldn't find you."

"If anyone asks, tell them that you were severally drunk and asked me to take you to your room. I, being nice, decided to stay with you do no one took advantage of you."

"I was drunk and I had Apollo take me to my room... He stayed with me so nothing would happen to me."

Hades could've sworn her voice broke slightly as she spoke of Apollo.

"Did anything happen?" Hades asked carefully.

Katherine took a breath, looked Hades straight in the eye, and said, "Nothing happened."

They sat in silence for a while, before Hades had to go back. He said goodbye to Katherine, and once he was alone, he called Hermes.

"What is it now, uncle," the god asked, annoyed at the call.

"I need you to tell Apollo that I'll be paying a visit later today. Someone I know has had something happen to her, and she was with Apollo last. He might know something."

"Alright, fine. But you owe me." Hermes hung up.

Hades had to be carefully with this. Apollo, despite his innocent looks, was a monster; a manipulative monster. He would know if Hades was trying something.

If Hades was right, Apollo would have evidence somewhere in his home. Hades just had to find it.

CHAPTER 11

"To tell you the truth, I wasn't expecting you to see me, uncle," Apollo said, taking a seat in a worn out leather chair. Hades sat opposite of his nephew, his body tense.

Apollo's home was very modern with windows instead of walls, modern decor, and open spacing. It looked like a condo you would see on a beach in California, not on the mountain side in Olympus. It was supposed to feel welcoming, but to Hades, he felt suffocated.

Hades plan was to find any digital devices Apollo might of used during the ball to see if he had anything with Katherine in it. He was incredible with technology, even if he was old fashioned.

In his cloak was his helmet of darkness. The helmet gave Jim the ability to travel into the show realm. The shadow realm was very similar to the real world, but time is different. Two hours in the shadow realm equaled one second in the real world. And objects could transfer between the realms, meaning that if you took an object in the shadows, it was gone in the other realm.

All Hades had to do was have Apollo go to another room, entering show realm, and collect the evidence. He had a flash drive to use on the devices to get the pictures. Apollo would notice something missing; it was better to leave things ad they were after getting what you need.

"So, tell me the reason behind this lovely visit."

"Do you remember a human girl under my care, Katherine Bakers?"

"The human you took under. Yes, I remember her. Beautiful little creature." Hades saw lust flash in Apollo's eyes. He tried to relax his tense body.

"Someone has hurt her. She won't tell anyone. Her sister is convinced it was one of the people she talked to at the ball."

"How do you know I was one of them?"

"It's my kingdom; I know everything. Now, do you have any ideas as to what could've possibly happen?"

Apollo shook his head. "No. I was with her. She asked me to take her to her room, and I stayed to make sure no one bothered her."

"Did anyone seem to take a liking to her at the ball? You seemed to be with her the longest."

Apollo raised his brow. "What are you accusing? That I did something to your human?"

Hades growled. "She isn't 'my human.'"

"Tell me, uncle: why are you do interested with her? Do you tend to replace Persephone's empty spot next to you with her?"

Hades fisted his hands, his nails digging into his palm. He had to keep his cool. He knew Apollo was trying to provoke him with Persephone, he knew what will happen to Hades if he doesn't find a queen. Everyone knew.

Hades knew Katherine wasn't ready. She had potential, but she wasn't ready. Hades couldn't even describe his feelings for her. They were so foreign to him, he forgot what it was like to feel.

With Katherine, he felt somewhat free. It made him happy to see her smile. He didn't want her miserable. He cared for her, even if he hid it. Could Zeus be right after all? Was Katherine the one?

"Persephone is in no context of this conversation."

Apollo chuckled. "Alright, alright. I didn't see any suspicious behavior from the guests. But you know I wasn't the only to see her."

But you were the one that had an extreme interest in her.

"I'm getting a drink. Want one?"

"Surprise me."

Apollo stood up and walked into the kitchen.

This was this it, his moment.

Hades snuck the helmet from out of his cloak and slipped it on his head.

All light disappeared and was replaced by dark shadows. Time moved much slower here.

Hades swiftly moved around the livingroom, peaking through crooks. The selves were clear and every known hiding spot was clear.

Hades moved to the upstairs into Apollo's room. The room was clean and neat, a desk sitting in the corner with a laptop opened. Hades moved to the laptop and looked through files. There were some that showed explicit scenes with other girls, but so far, none of Katherine.

He closed the files and looked through other devices. There was digital cameras and multiple phones in drawers in the desk. Like the laptop, there were other girls, but not Katherine.

There was one last phone in the bottom of the drawer. Hades looked through the phone and immediately, his blood ran cold.

Her body was bare.

Her body covered in red bite marks.

Her hair a tangled mess.

Her face red from tears.

It was true. Apollo raped her and took pictures.

Rage flooded through him as he went through the photos. They were in different angles, some even in the act. And in each photo, she was crying.

He took out the drive, and downloadee to photos. This was his evidence.

Putting everything back in place, Hades rushed back downstairs and sat on his seat. He store the drive in his pocket and quickly took of the helmet, shoving it under his cloak.

Apollo reappeared with two drinks in his hand. He handed one to Hades, not even knowing that Hades had the photos of what he done to Katherine.

"There's are the photos, yes?"

Athena looked at the pictures, her expression grim and her lips in a thin line. She has seen pictures like this, but what Apollo did was gruesome.

She swiped the screen, seeing more pictures. She had to bite a gasp back when she saw the last one.

Poor child, she thought. Her innocence taken too soon.

"Has she told anyone about the..."

Hades shook his head. "Her sister said she acted like she was in a depressive episode."

Rage flowed through his veins. A part of him wanted to tear Apollo apart. But another was disappointed in him. Katherine was under his care; he should've known. He knew Apollo was a monster, and didn't tell Katherine to stay away. He felt responsible; it was because of him she was raped and lost her innocence.

"I'll report it to the Council and make a case. Katherine will need to testify."

Katherine awoke from a nightmare, sweat beating down her forehead. Her sheets were wet from the sweat and her gown clung to her.

Flashes of Apollo came to her mind, of him on top of her, marking her.

She whimpered and cried, trying to force the memories back.

Suddenly, she felt arms around her. Her adrenaline was through the roof, and she struggled against whoever held her.

"Katherine, it's me."

"Hades?"

She knew it was him, before she asked the question. But with Apollo fresh in her mind, for a split moment, she thought Hades was him.

"Hades..."

"I know about Apollo."

Katherine gasped. "H-How?"

"I went to his home in Olympus, and...saw the photos."

It was then that Katherine broke down. Her body shook as she sobbed. Hades arms tightened around her, his chest against her back.

He whispered to her, trying to calm her down. He swayed their bodies side to side in a soothing rocking motion.

"Why didn't you tell me?"

"I c-couldn't. He told me n-no one would believe me. A-And I would never be worthy of you."

A low growl ripped through Hades chest. He turned Katherine around and placed both of her hands on her shoulders.

"I would never think that. Apollo is a monster! I may hide it, but I care for you, Katherine. I can't explain it, but I care about you."

Tears streamed down her face. She had never heard some-one saying they cared, not even from her parents. Namie cared, of course, but Hades was different. He made her feel something, she felt free with him, happy even. It was easy to talk to him.

He terrified her at the start, but through that exterior, he cared.

The thought made her heart skip a beat.

"Hades?"

"Yes?"

"W-Will you stay with me tonight? I don't want to be alone."

Hades nodded, not even thinking about it. He moved the covers and tucked himself and Katherine in, her head on his chest.

This feels right, they both thought before they drifted off to sleep.

CHAPTER 12

Faint light slivered through the curtains, the breeze slightly chilled as it always was. Katherine shivered and snuggled into something warm, a small smile on her face. Her arm and leg was wrapped around something hard yet soft. It didn't register that she was wrapped around the God of the Dead.

Hades was still wide awake, his mind buzzing from the events of yesterday. How was he supposed to tell Katherine that she had to testify in front of his family about what happened? She was petrified of telling anyone; even her own sister.

He was still angry at himself. He should've protected her from his nephew. A small part of him hoped that Apollo wouldn't come, or it he did, not take an interest in the human. But no... Apollo did much worse to her.

Seeing her cry before she passed out from exhaustion made him stir in every emotion. Sadness, anger, revenge, pity...and scared.

The fearful Hades, God of the Dead, was scared.

He was scared because she would revert back to her shell.

He was scared that she would see him and all the other Olympians as monsters.

He was scared of losing her.

Hades was scared of losing Katherine.

That was what both frightened and confused him the most. Katherine was a mere human with a troubled past of living in the shadows of her own mind and her sister.

Hades knew all too well on what that was like.

Despite being one of the older and original gods, he had always felt shadowed by his brothers. No mortal liked a god in charge of the dead. Except...maybe Katherine.

He felt Katherine stir beside him, bringing herself closer to him, her arm and leg wrapped around him. The god's face flushed red, something abnormal to him, as she snuggled into his side, a small smile on her face.

Hades took the moment to see her.

She looks so peaceful, he thought to himself. Even with the dried tear streaks on her cheeks, she looked beautiful. Her long black hair looked soft and thick enough to run his fingers through, her pale skin seeming to glow in the morning light. The long night shirt went to down mid-thigh, which gave him a view of her legs.

Hades saw a few of the painful red bite marks from Apollo against her pale skin, sticking out like a sore thumb. They were scattered all over, most of them in her inner thight close to her core.

It took all of his restrant to not want to do something to Apollo. Athena said that he could not do anything to Apollo until she has looked through the photos, met with the Counsel, and arranged the court. Hades knew better than to mess with a goddess of war and justice. Even though he had much more power than her, he would never win against her.

He moved the covers to cover up her legs, and carefully got out of the bed. Katherine stirred, causing Hades to stop. He didn't even breathe, afraid that even a breath would wake her. When she didn't wake, he realised his breath and got out of the bed.

He instantly missed the warmth of her body against his. He resisted the urge to get back under the covers with her.

Before he left, he placed a gentle kiss on the human's forehead, his lips lingering on her skin more than normal.

When he left, he missed the huge smile on Katherine's face.

All day, Hades had some of the maids check in on Katherine. He could've used Namie, but the older sister didn't know about the rape. That was something Katherine would tell on her own time.

The maids reported back that Katherine seemed well considering. She was eating some. But all throughout the day, she had this small twinkle in her eyes, one so small, one might not notice it. But if you looked really close, you could see it.

Hades wondered if Katherine knew that he stayed with her throughout the night, felt the hesitation when he got out of the bed, and the lingering kiss on her forehead.

The god knew she was no way near ready for anything intimate, so he knew he had to put all of his growing feelings for the girl on the back burner until she said so.

He needed to get a handle on his emotions. He hadn't felt anything since Persephone's passing. Even though she was a goddess, she chose death with a mortal than to be with Hades. It had taken a toll on the god, making his heart stop cold in mid beating.

At first, he ran everything smoothily with the help on Charos and Hermes with the sortment of the dead. But soon, more and more people began dying. Everything was getting out of control. The stress had caused the god to stop rational thinking and decided on whatever afterlife he chose for the soul.

No soul had a fair trial, souls were confused as religions became more complex as more of them appeared.

Without Persephone, he couldn't do the one thing right.

The three brothers needed queens to help keep their rein in check. Zeus has Hera; Poseidon has Amphitrite; Hades.. .had Persephone.

Seeing Katherine on Persephone's throne during the ball made Hades think that maybe, Katherine was the one that his brother's hoped for. Despite her inner darkness, she was kind to the servents and nymphs; every time she came into the throne room, the souls looked at her in admiration; and already, his nephews and nieces were placing bets on when their uncle would do something...not if.

The thought of Katherine sitting on the throne next to his made his heart skip a beat. She looked like she was born to sit on it. It was like she was born to lead.

Hades knew that he didn't have much time left before his existence disappeared. Hopefully Katherine would be the one that would put him back together.

CHAPTER 13

Katherine sat in the maze, Cerberus curled in a little ball on her lap. He was so adorable; how could human's imagine this cute little ball as a massive monster that should be feared?

The smile on her face was still etched onto her face from this morning, the place where Hades kissed her still warm. At first she thought she imagined it, but when she felt his lips linger on her forehead, she realized it wasn't a dream.

He had stayed the entire night with her, holding her until she fell alseep, and even then, he never left. She wondered if he slept at all during the night, or stayed awake.

She didn't blame him for staying up.

Yesterday was intense for the both of them. Hades had found the photos Apollo had took of her. She thought that he would see her as used. But he didn't.

The look of hurt on his face when she never told him what happened, but the smoldering anger that burned in his black eyes. It was like coal burning; cold at first but it instantly burned the moment you lit it.

Katherine has never seen someone feel that much for her. No one ever really noticed her, not even her parents. She had never seen such an intense emotion before in someone.

In a strange way, it made her happy that someone did care for her. And out of all people, it was a god who ruled over the dead.

Cerberus yawned and stirred on her lap, letting out a soft howl. Katherine giggled at the pup before setting him down back on the ground.

"Ready to go back?" The small pup yipped in delight, jumping around on it's paws. Katherine got off the bench, dusted off her dress, and followed Cerberus out of the maze and into the garden.

The garden never ceased to amaze her. Jeweled flowers glistened in the light, a rainbow of colors cascading on the path. They were all colors from vivid red to the brightess white crystals. Katherine adored them all, but her favorite was one near the fountain.

It was a dark blue crystal that, in the light, glistened with a mulitude of colors, some that she never heard of. But during the night, it looked black as coal that sparkled in dim light. One of the nymphs told her that that crystal flower was the master's favorite. He had it planted soon after Persephone arrived to the Underworld during her first winter.

A pang of jealousy coursed through her when the nymph told her that it too was Persephone's favorite. By the way the maids and nymphs spoke of her almost seemed...sad and confused. Whenever she asked what happened to the goddess, everyone dodged it and went on their way.

Could she have possibly died, she thought. But how? She's an immortal goddess.

Whatever happened, it took a toll on the kingdom and Hades.

The pup yipped at the girl, tugging on the hem of her dress. She snapped out of her thoughts quickly, shaking her head to get rid of those thoughts. It was stupid of her to be jealous of a goddess. Katherine would never be able to compare to Persephone.

Even if she tried...

Like usual, Katherine went to visit Hades in the throne room. Despite the weird looks from the souls, she didn't mind being there. Most of them were nice and friendly, while there were some that...weren't. She tried to stay away from those souls.

While on her way to the throne room, Katherine heard hushed whispered from behind a closed door. She remembered that it was some type of meeting room on her tour of the castle.

Her curiousity peaked a little when she heard Hades' familiar monotone voice. It was evident that he was angry about something from the way he tried to keep his voice down. There was another voice, female. Katherine didn't recognize the voice, but by the way she spoke told Katherine that she wasn't one to mess with.

Her curiousity got the better of her, and before Katherine knew it, her ear was pressed against the dense and cold door.

"What do you mean the Counsel denied assempling the court?" Hades voice strained to keep his voice down.

"I mean, they turned a blind eye to what happened." The female voice bit back.

Wait... Was this woman one of the goddesses? How did she know about Apollo?

Katherine tried to think about her times in the library, reading about some of the goddesses before the ball. Only one came to mind: a goddess of law and justice; Athena.

The woman was Athena.

"It's your word against Apollo, depsite the evidence you have. They won't assemble the court because they need to have her bring it to them, not you. They feel that you are accusing him in spite for--"

"I am not!" That time, Hades didn't bother keeping it quiet. "You saw those photos. She is still covered with those marks. Do they think I did all of that?"

"Some do, but like you, they don't approve of Apollo's activites with humans. Even Zeus isn't as bad anymore. I want Katherine to get justice for what happened to her, I really do. I can try to convice them to reconsider, but I can only do so much."

It grew quiet.

Katherine backed away from the door, the floor creaking under her weight. She froze, afraid that the gods in that room heard her.

The large wooden doors open, Hades standing in the doorway. His gaze softened when he saw Katherine, her face in disbelief. Hee hadn't meant for her to hear that. He knew that he misused her trust to tell Athena, but she knew more about this than he did. It seemed logical to him.

But it wasn't that; it was disbelief for the fact that no one was doing anything to help. Only Hades and Athena was doing something. The others decided to turn a blind eye, thinking that it was just another stupid girl that Apollo had for the night.

"Katherine..."

"No one believes us," she said, her voice cracking. "Your family doesn't believe me."

"I'm sorry."

They stood there, not speaking. The air was thick between them as they both got lost in their own thoughts.

Katherine wanted to cry and curl up in a ball; Hades wanted to comfort her so he could take her pain away.

He wanted to so badly. He just wanted to hold her like he did last night. It physically hurt him to see her like this; in the dark ll by herself with no one. No one deserves to live like that.

"Hades..."

He barely heard her tiny voice. It wavered and shook as she tried to control her emotions. What surprised him was when she held out her arms, like she wanted to be embraced.

He didn't hesitate.

Hades wrapped his arms around her, stroking her long hair. She sobbed in his chest, her whole body shaking. His arms tightened around her.

"We'll figure this out," Hades whispered to her. "I promise."

Katherine nodded. She pulled away enough for her to see Hades. She knew her eyes were puffy and red, but she didn't care.

In that moment, her feelings for the god only grew. It was only a matter of time before she would do something.

Or if he will do something...

CHAPTER 14

Hecate, like usual, stayed in her little office near the far end of the library. Candles floated around the small room, the multitude of crystals casting a range of colors across the dark room.

The goddess sat in the middle of the room, her eyes closed as she spoke the spell in her native tongue. Some of her followers had broken a sacred rule; it only seem fit to punish them for it.

As she spoke the spell, the candles flickered as the energy in the room grew darker and sinister. Hecate felt the darkness grow stronger inside her, slowly overtaking the good in her.

When she came to the last part of the spell, she felt the darkness explode within her, blowing out the candles. She sat there in the dark as the spell traveled to those who broke the rules. Slowly, the darkness began to retreat deep inside her, balancing itself with the light.

Standing up, she relit the candles before leaving the room, casting a spell so no one got in. Anyone naive in the ways of magic and witchcraft would cause chaos, making an inbalance in the world of light and dark.

This is what Hecate did. She oversaw good and evil so that they remained balance. Every good person had an evil person to counter-balance.

But that wasn't the only thing. She helps oversee the Underworld with Hades, making sure that the good and evil were placed in their proper resting place. She was in charge over the ghosts that stayed in the castle, as well as the hell-hounds that guarded the perimeter of the Underworld and Tartarus.

She didn't mind it. Most time, she spent her days in her room, overseeing the balance.

Locking the door for safe measures, Hecate placed the key around her neck.

The cavern outside was dark, the favorite time for Hecate. This was when the darkness inside was itching to get out. It craved to be a part of the night, but she controlled herself.

"I wonder if that girl is still here."

The human girl, Katherine Bakers, fascinated her. Lord Hades had never taken in a girl before, not since Persephone. She had noticed the way that Hades started treating the girl after the first week. She knew that the front when they met was a scare; he was like a teddy bear.

The front was because of Persephone. She had made him so happy in the beginning. He made sure she was happy, allowing her to turn part of the castle and the garden into something she was proud of. But when she met that human man and decided to follow him in death, it tore the god in two.

She wondered if Katherine knew that she was staying in Persephone's old room?

It also intrigued her that Katherine held a resemblance to the late goddess. They both had the long, dark hair; the same innocent eyes; even the same body type. Only, Katherine was filled with an inner darkness that seemed to overfill, yet she never thought about herself.

Hecate knew about the girl from hearing her thoughts before she came to the Underworld. The darkness inside that girl was overbearing. Seeing her own sister murdered, her parents negleting her for years... It even made the fearful Goddess of Witchcraft feel pity for the human.

But Katherine was still good. Despite the hardships and trauma, she still cared for others, even if she didn't want to show it.

She was like Lord Hades.

They were good for each other. Hopefully, they realize that before their demons separated them.

Leaving the library, Hecate began to trudge her way to her chamber. It was dead silent, no servants or nymphs in the hallways. The silence was something Hecate was use to, but normally there was some noise and activity.

Shaking her head, she ignored it before continuing her way.

When she arrived at her chamber, something made her stop cold in her steps. The hairs stood on the back of her neck. Whatever was around her, was something that made the goddess hesitate.

She hurried into her room, quickly closing the door behind her. She realised a shaky breath, relaxing against the door.

Suddenly, there was a blast of bright light, as bright as the sun. Hecate hissed at the light, shielding her eyes. The light burned before dimming down. Hecate uncovered her eyes to see Apollo standing in the middle of the room, a crooked smile on his face.

Hecate never liked Apollo. He was too arrogant and cocky for his own good, going out to the mortal world to find a new girl to create new heroes. She never knew why he was obssessed with an heir.

"Hecate," Apollo greeted. "It's been a while."

"Here I was hoping to never see your smug face again."

Apollo placed his hand over his heart, pretending to be hurt. "I'm offended, Hecate."

"Why are you here?"

He chuckled. "I'm sure you're aware of the human, Katherine." She nodded. "And I'm sure you know a certain...taintn ess around her now, right?"

Hecate glared at the god. Of course she knew what happened. When she looked at Katherine's energy, it was tainted and violated. Images of red sores against pale skin, the flash of a camera... She knew it was Apollo who had took advantage of the girl. It made her blood boil.

"And that her feelings for my uncle are growing."

"Why are you here?"

"You're the Goddess of Magic and Witchcraft... So you know spells."

Hecate did not like where this is going...

"I want you to cast a spell on Katherine; one to make her mine to possess."

CHAPTER 15

Katherine's fingers skimmed over the old and weathered keys on the piano.

It had been years since she has touched piano keys. They were old and a shade of yellow instead of a pearly white. Despite how old it was, she could still feel the uses it had, even if no one used it for a while.

No one knew that Katherine could play the piano. It was a natural talent that she kept hidden from everyone. Even Namie didn't know.

Namie didn't know a lot about her younger sister now. She didn't know that Katherine knew how to ballroom dance or play the piano. She liked it like that.

While stumbling around looking for somewhere else to spend her time besides the library and garden, she accidentily found a room at the far end of an emoty corridor. It was evident that no one came down the corridor.

It felt sad, going down that corridor. The darkness down that hall felt sad. Like it had been abandoned for years and years until Katherine rediscovered it.

The room that the piano was in was very spacious, the walls mostly made of tall mirrors with high ceilings. There were chandeliers hanging above, casting elegant shawdows across the room. Katherine noticed that on the far wall, there were two grand French doors that lead out to a big balconey and staircase down to the gardens.

Katherine had left open the French doors to let in a light breeze from the cavern.

Taking a deep breath, Katherine began to play one of her favorite songs she listened to back home.

"Would you bled for me?

Lick it off my lips like you needed me?

Would you sit me on the couch with your fingers in my mouth?

You look so cool when you're reading me."

Katherine bobbed her head to the beat of the piano, her fingers moving along the piano keys, hitting them like butterfly kisses.

"But I've got my mind made up this time,

'Cause there's a menace in my bed,

Can you see his silhouette?

Can you see his silhouette?

Can you see his silhouette?

And I've got my mind made up this time,

Go on and light a cigarette,

Set a fire in my head, set a fire in my head tonight."

Katherine continued to sing and play, the noise echoing in the spaceous room. She was lost in the music as it flowed oh so easily through her.

It reminded her of the times when she would go to her tutor's home for hours, telling her parents that she was at the library studying, while in fact she was learning to play piano. She had never felt so free before. Only the piano gave her that type of freedom that she longed for. She longed to be free from the darkness in her heart, to move passed the trauma.

In the weeks that she was here, most of the time, she forgot about her parents and Namie's murderer. Those things that plagued her mind wasn't there all the time like before. In a way, she escaped those physical demons that haunted her.

They were still there, scratching at the back of her head. But now, she didn't fear them as much.

Hades was around to protect her.

Protecting her. Why did that thought make her feel giddy inside?

"Don't forget me, don't forget me.

I wouldn't leave you if you'd let me.

When you met me, when you met me,

Don't forget me, don't forget me.

I wouldn't leave you if you'd--"

"I didn't know you could play."

Katherine haulted, her fingers stopping in mid air. She didn't realize that Hades was behind her until she felt his breath on the back of her neck. It's warmth tickled the skin, leaving goosebumps.

"You sound beautifly. I've only heard a few voices like yours in my lifetime."

Katherine blushed at the compliment. Her body began to feel warm as Hades leaned closer, his chest in her back.

"Can you continue?"

Nodding, Katherine began again, trying to control the shaking in her hands.

But I've got my mind made up this time,

'Cause there's a menace in my bed,

Can you see his silhouette?

Can you see his silhouette?

Can you see his silhouette?

And I've got my mind made up this time,

Go on and light a cigarette,

Set a fire in my head, set a fire in my head tonight, tonight, tonight."

Katherine continued to play a few notes and finally ended the song.

She looked over her shoulder, and nearly jumped out of her seat to see his face very close to hers. Up close, Katherine could see all the small details on his face: a few white scars that dotted his face, how his black eyes had more dimension that just black. They were so captivating to look at, you couldn't look away.

Though it was embarassing for her, every night, she always had his eyes on her mind. She constantly saw them in her dreams, and whenever she woke up, all she wanted was to go back to sleep to see them a little more.

"Dance with me."

"W-What?"

Hades chuckled. "Dance. With. Me."

"What about the music?"

"I'll take care of that."

He held out his hand, waiting for her to take it. He saw her hesitate, but she did take it. Hades took them to the center of the room.

Hades placed his hands on her waist while she wrapped her wrists around his neck. He gently pulled her closer to him before swaying side to side. Music soon began to play as a spirit of a musican sat at the piano.

Katherine's face was burning hot from being close to the god. At the ball, she didn't experience this: it was a formal ball and their dance was only professional. Now, that they were alone, it was very...intimate.

Her heart was beating out of her chest as they danced. The music was slow and soft, like their dance.

After a while, Hades sped up the pace, widening their strides. Katherine followed with a great deal of elegance, the fact that she took ballroom slipped the god's mind. Hades began to dance them around the room, Katherine following his lead.

It warmed his heart to see her smile as they danced, her cheerful laugh that echoed. She looked so beautiful when she smiled.

When the song was near the end, Hades did something daring and dipped Katherine, holdin her body flush against him to not drop her. Katherine held on tightly as her body was bent backwards and suspended above the ground.

It was like time seemed to stop right then as they held onto each other, the spirit gone and the room now silent, the only sound was the beating of their hearts.

Hades took a risk and glanced at her pink lips, his mind instantly imagining how they would feel against his, how she tasted.

Instantly, Hades no longer saw Katherine, he saw Persephone. Her hair was down, long and flowy with a small flower crown on her head. She wore a pale pink dress with a loose sweetheart neckline outlined with lace. Her doe like eyes stared up at him with such love and devotion, before she found love in another man.

"Persephone...?"

Persephone didn't answer. The look in her eyes soon went to one of confusion. "Hades?"

Wait, that's not her voice... That's not Persephone's voice.

"Hades."

Hades blinked and shook his head. Katherine looked up at him, trying to hide the hurt when he called her Persephone at such an intimate moment.

Hades realized what happened and quickly pulled her back up with him, backing away from her. His eyes burned with tears as memories of Persephone bombarded his mind. The girl in front of him blurred between Katherine and Persephone.

Why did they have to look the same?! Why are the Fates so cruel to me?

"I'm sorry."

Hades left without saying a word, not wanting Katherine to see him breaking down; he never saw the tears stream down Katherine's face.

He still loves her, Katherine thought bitterly. He still loves her; he'll never get over her.

She knew it was stupid to think Hades had the same feelings for her. He was only replicating it all out of pity, maybe as an apology for being so hostile to her the first day they met.

"I'm so stupid." She cursed herself, sitting back on the piano bench. Her body shook as sobs took over her body.

She really was a naive little human.

If she only knew that Apollo was in the castle, forcing Hestia to do his bidding.

Apollo stood against the wall in the small room, watching intently as Hestia sat in the circle, pictures of Katherine littering the outer circle. Apollo knew that Hades would take the evidence to show to Athena, but Apollo was smarter.

"Hurry it up, Hestia. You know I won't hesitate to bring Aeetes, Kirke and Medea, and Aigialeus into this."

Hecate growled when Apollo threatened her husband and children.

No matter how much she wanted Katherine to be with Hades, she had to protect her family.

Hecate tried to relax, concentrating on the image of Katherine and Apollo together. Speaking in her native tongue, the energy in the room began to shift. It grew darker and colder as the Hecate commended the darkness to go after Katherine.

She felt the darkness leave her, swarming around the room. Apollo swore as the darkness circled him like a hungry python.

"Go and do your bidding on the human Katherine Bakers... Make her Apollo's and his only. Only Apollo and I can break the bond."

Hecate opened her eyes, her eyes pitch black like a demons. She looked at the swirl of darkness that was around Apollo and hissed at it. "Make her his!"

The darkness shreaked before slivering through the crack at the bottom of the door.

The swirl moved fastly from the library to where Katherine was in the music room.

Katherine heard a high pitched scream from the door. She looked up in fear to see a large mass of darkness coming towards her.

Before she could even scream, the darkness charged at her, entering her open mouth and into her soul and body. Katherine cried and screamed as she felt the darkness grow and grow, pushing at every corner of her mind with its scream.

Her body jolted and convulsed as the darkness possessed every part of her. She screamed and cried for Hades to come. But the longer she screamed, he never came.

As soon as the darkness arrived, the chaos stopped. Katherine felt extremely different, like it wasn't even her own body.

She fell to the floor.

Her once blue eyes were pitch black, soulless.

She was unrecognizable.

Hecate took a deep breath, feeling the darkness course through the human. "It's done. The darkness will slowly break her apart so it doesn't look suspious. It'll be about a month before it's complete... Only you and I can stop it before it's complete."

"Oh, I won't be stopping it no time soon."

"You never told me why you wanted her. She's a simple human."

Apollo chuckled darkly. "If you only knew her future and potential."

Hades quickly ran to the music room, the sound of Katherine's scream echoing through his brain. He made it to the room to find Katherine on the floor unconscious. Fear coursed through his veins as he rushed to him as he rushed to her side.

He stopped once he felt the strong darkness surrounding her body and soul. It was thick and dark like tar. He didn't know who summoned the darkness, whoever sent it to her covered their tracks.

He was gonna protect her. He promised himself that he was going to protect her in a way that he couldn't with Persephone.

Now someone had possessed her, and he didn't know why or how.

CHAPTER 16

All she could hear was a constant buzzing in her head.

All she felt was her body suspended through a thick darkness.

All she saw was just darkness, shadows dancing around her in a menacing dance.

Voices spoke to her, their voices sounding demonic. She heard her mother's voice, telling her that she was nothing more than a mistake. She heard her father, shouting curses. She heard Namie, who reminded her that she was in the shadows and would remain there even in death.

She heard Hades, reminding her that he could only have his heart on Persephone, and that any kindness he showed her was out of pity.

Katherine wanted to cry, to scream, to stop the constant buzzing and voices that seemed to forever screaming at her. The more she tried to resist, the more the noise got louder.

She had no time of what was going around her. She didn't know that she was unconscious on the floor, in Hades' arms.

"Katherine," Hades pleaded, gently shaking her. She remained limp in his arms, her skin a sickly shade of white. Her body would twitch, but nothing more. He had no idea that her soul was swallowed by the darkness, being replaced by the spell itself.

Hades could feel her soul, but it was so far in the darkness he could only feel the moving shadows.

He had no idea that Katherine was in her own hell, in eternal darkness with the voices of her loved ones confirming her worse fears as reality, no matter how much she knew it was true, their words still pierced through her heart.

Hades had never felt so much fear since Persephone's passing. Then, he had somehwat control. Now, all he could do was wait until she woke up.

Having Katherine limp against him brought back memories of that day centuries ago...

No matter how hard Hades tried, Persephone was set on her decision. Seeing her on the bed, all dressed in white with flowers weaved through her hair, made his once beating heart ache.

Everyone had left after Hades did what he did. It wss only respectful for Hades to spend a few moments alone with his dead wife.

Never in his eons of life, would he had thought he would kill the one who he loved. He was always surrounded by death, that was something he was used to. Persephone brought life to her stays in the winter. Now that she was gone, he felt the coldness from before leak through.

It was no secret about their unhappiness in the past few centuries. No one wanted to mention the acticites Persephone did during her time back home. Hades did tell her she could do whatever she wanted up above; she took that advice.

Hades didn't know about the affair when he met the soul while Persephone was in the Underworld. The look of confusion and astounisment the man had when he saw Persephone told Hades one thing; that man was her lover.

No wonder she was so eager to go back home every spring. Of course she was always eager to go back home, but she found beauty and contentment in the land of the dead.

It hurt. The pain and knowledge that she no longer loved him. But when she asked him to do the unthinkable, it was too much.

For days, the earth was reighned with shadows and demons that possessed innocent humans, destroying everything. There were earthquakes and volcanos erupted, the most famous one in Pompeii. But that didn't matter. Hades unleashed hell on earth.

Zeus and Posideon tried to calm their brother, but it was no use. Only when Persephone talked to him, Hades knew that he had to let her go. She was growing unhappy. She wanted to die as a human with the man she found love in.

They always say that if you love something, you set it free.

And that's what Hades did.

He freed Persephone by death.

It felt like an eternality until Hades felt Katherine stir. He watched as she blinked and hissed at the sudden light in the room.

She felt unnaturally cold, colder than death. Hades saw that her vivid blue eyes that he grew to love were now like his; black as coal. They were dark and cold and empty.

Hades was not an expert in witchcraft and magic, but he knew that depending on the spell, meant possession. The darkness in her soul was meant to change her emotions, to break down her soul until she submited to the darkness.

Hecate knew about magic. Maybe she would know what this darkness was, if it can be broken, and why.

"Hades..."

Her voice was quiet and small, like she had just spent hours screaming and crying.

Hades knew that her soul was stuck in the darkness. Right now, beside her eyes, she was fine. He knew that it would take time for the spell to be complete. For now, he needed to make sure that he found a way to stop it before whoever made it got what they wanted from her.

He moved a stray hair from her forehead, which glistened in sweat. It ws gentle, almost like he was too scared to touch her in fear she would break. In some ways, she might.

Katherine realised a shaky breath, trying to control her heartbeat. She felt different, like she didn't recoginzed her own body. The darkness inside her was stirring around inside of her mind; she could feel it.

"Hades... I feel it... Inside."

"I know," he whispered. "It's a spell."

"Hades..."

"I'm sorry for leaving you alone. If I didn't leave, I could've saved you. Now..."

Katherine smiled, though it was sad. "It's okay. I get it... You love Persephone."

Hades wanted to correct her, but he knew it was true. He still loved his dead wife.

But now...with his feelings for Katherine...it was hard to see anything other than the human girl.

CHapter 17

How can you describe the fact that your soul is being devoured to a literal darkness? A manifestation of shadows conjured by someone obssessed with you, for reasons still unknown?

When Hades asked her how it felt, Katherine couldn't describe it. How could she say that she felt her soul in something thick and black, voices scratching at her mind; voices of her mom, dad, sister, and... Hades himself.

She couldn't tell him that she kept hearing his voice inside her mind. Full of malice and spite as he screamed that he would never love her, that it was all for pity.

That hurt the most.

Katherine always knew. When the servants and nympths dodged the question, why he had seemed happy looking at the diamond throne...calling out her name when they danc ed... She knew, it was obvious.

She doesn't know how Persephone died, but she had a feeling Hades had something to do with it.

Hades gently picked her up, placing her back on the bench. He kneeled down in front of her: even when he was on his knees, he towered over her. Her eyes went back to their natural blue color, but they were still somehow darker than before. Dark and dead.

She had visibly calmed down, no longer shaking, but there was still fear in her eyes. She kept whispering to herself, some of it nonsense.

This was a common sign of a spell possession. Though it had been eons since Hades saw a human possessed by such a spell, it has happened.

"How are you feeling?" He asked her, his voice barely a whisper.

"Fine... Just different."

He nodded. He would have to tell her older sister what happened to Katherine. She already didn't much care for the god, though his intentions were good. Knowing the fact that Namie accused him of raping Katherine, she would believe that Hades was the one who casted the spell.

But Hades knew little to nothing about magic and witchcraft. He didn't conjure such things. That was Hecate's domain.

Hecate! Maybe she could help.

"Are you okay to walk?"

"I think so?"

Katherine began to get off the bench, her legs wobbily. Her body was still weak from the attack. Hades wrapped one of his arms around her waist, holding her close to his body. Her body temperature was cooler than before. Hades would never admit it in front of her, but her warmth made his heart skip a few beats.

The god and the human walked together to the library, the silence thick between them. Hades was worried about trying to find a way to break the spell: Katherine was thinking about when he called her Persephone.

She knew it was going to happen at some point. From the side glances and hushed whispers, she knew that everyone in or around the castle was curious as to why she was here.

During her first few days here in the Underworld, she heard two maids outside her room talking to each other.

"She looks so much like the late Queen," one of the maids commented. "I mean, they almost look identical. You don't think that human is somehow her sister?"

"I doubt it," the other maid said. "She could be a reincarnation of Persephone."

"Probably, seems more likely."

Katherine had no idea on how much she resembled the goddess until she researched the Goddess of Spring one day in the library.

Persephone had long, flowy black hair, pale olive skin, and blue eyes that were as blue as a clear spring sky. In the picture, the girl looked no older than nineteen, standing in a field of flowers. She wore a long, light pink toga with a rose crown on top of her head. She was beautiful; no wonder Hades fell in love with her.

The picture was before she came to the Underworld. The next one that Katherine saw, it was of Hades and Persephone. Hades stood behind his wife, ine of his hands on her shoulder. They both had bright and matching smiles.

They looked to be a perfect couple.

It was at that point that Katherine was envious of the young goddess. The girl was the picture of perfection, even being compared to Aphrodite.

Seeing that picture only made Katherine's mouth bitter with jealousy.

They came to the library, and walked to the very back to a tiny room in the corner. The door was heavily locked with several padlocks. Katherine could feel the darkness surrounding that room, but...there was something else. There seemed to be other energy; it felt pure, good.

She remebered reading that Hecate was both good and evil, as the representation of balance. She was the keeper of the hell-hounds, as well as she was the mother of witchcraft.

Hades knocked on the door, but didn't get an answer. He knew that she spent most of the night in that room as her powers were stronger during those late hours.

"Hecate," Hades called out, but once again, he never heard a reply. Growing a little impatient, Hades tore the locks off the door and kicked the door open with his boot.

The room was empty and dark.

Panic coursed through him as he realized that Hecate wasn't here. He tried to sense her energy, but nothing came up. Almost like she placed a block between herself and Hades.

How was Hades supposed to know how to break the spell? Katherine was possessed and he had no idea what the spell was or when it would be complete.

He sighed, feeling completely frustrated. Hecate still had to be in the castle; he just had to find her.

He went back to Katherine, who was leaning against the wall, her body wary from trying to fight the spell. He knew that the spell will break her eventually and consume her. Hopefully she will fight long enough for Hades to find Hecate and stop the spell.

She looked exhausted. There were already circles under her eyes.

Katherine was too tired to notice that Hades had picked her up bridal style, his hand on her lower back and under her thighs. She didn't have the energy to blush or get flustered. On instinct, Katherine wrapped her arms around Hades' neck to keep herself from falling. She didn't notice that Hades heart skipped a few beats.

They made it to Katherine's chambers. Hades opened the door as best he could, and went inside. He gently laid her on the bed, and covered her with the comforter. She curled into the covers and quickly went to sleep.

Hades kicked off his boots and shrugged off his shirt before climbing into bed. He kept trying to convince himself he was only doing this to keep an eye on Katherine, but in reality, he liked sleeping next to her.

And even though Hades didn't want to admit it, he was falling for the human. Fast.

CHapTer 18

Katherine didn't sleep. The voices in her head wouldn't let her. Every time she closed her eyes, they screamed and shouted at her to wake up. She tossed and turned all night, trying not to wake Hades who ended up sleeping with her.

Before the sun came out, Katherine slipped out of bed and went out the balconey that was outside her room. The cavern was still dark and chilly. The flowers down at the garden below glistened in the dim lights coming from the windows.

Katherine sat down at the edge, her legs dangling over the edge, her dress flowing as she kicked her legs.

Her mind felt so chaotic right now; her thoughts and emotions jumbled up, voices of her loved ones constantly yelling at her. Hades voice was what tore her open the most. Her feelings for him have grown since the Hallows Eve Ball. That night was only a week ago, though it felt like an eternality ago.

It was funny how much she came to care for the immortal. She knew that at first, Hades was intimidating, as that was his front for everyone. But over the weeks, she saw through the facade and noticed that he was a caring person who had his heart crushed by his wife.

Katherine wanted to know how Persephone died. She knew that Hades had something to do with it, but that was something only Hades can share with her; if he decided to share his story.

She couldn't help but sigh.

She wondered how her parents were. Not only did they lose a daughter to an unknown murderer, but now she was missing too. Katherine doubted that her parents really cared. She was nineteen years old, she was an adult and could do whatever she wanted.

If that was the case, Katherine knew that they didn't bother with missing poster signs.

"Care if I join you?"

Katherine looked up to see a shirtless hades towering over her, his black hair ruffled from whatever sleep he had. Katherine nodded before looking away, not trusting her voice.

Should she mention the fact that he called her Persephone? Thinking back to that moment caused her heart string to contrast painfully in her chest.

Hades grunted as he sat next to her, swinging his legs over.

They sat in a tense silence, too obsorbed in their thoughts. Katherine wondered what was going through his mind. She wondered if Hades knew that, consciously or not, he called her his dead wife's name.

Hades cleared his throat. "So... How are you feeling?" Katherine shrugged. Hades could already tell by the circles under her eyes that the spell was already taking a huge toll her, and hasn't been a day yet.

Hades knew that she was restless. He felt her toss and turn in the covers, completely restless. Every time she would finally get comfortable, she would suddenly jolt like someone poured cold water on her. He knew that the voices in her head were the cause of it.

What he wouldn't give to take all her pain away.

He will kill whoever casted that spell onto her.

The sudden urge to touch her and comfort her was strong, too strong. All Hades wanted to do was to wrap her up in his arms and take away all the voices. He wanted to protect her from all the darkness. But it was hard to do so when it was inside.

He didn't even notice that his hand held her hand in his, the coolness of her skin against his. Katherine's breath hitched in her throat as Hades intertwined their fingers, holding onto her hand as if he was afraid of losing her.

When she tried to pull her hand back, thinking that Hades was doing it out of pity or mistook her as Persephone again, Hades didn't let go. In fact, he held her hand tighter.

He never said anything as to why: he just sat there, looking out at the dark cavern, holding her hand like she might slip through his fingers.

Her heart was pounding in her chest as they held hands. It strangely felt natural, like they did this a million times before.

"I'm sorry."

Katherine looked at Hades. "For what?"

"I called you Persephone back in when we danced." He sighed, the weight on his chest getting heavier. "You look so much like her, Katherine. I know you've heard everyone talk. And it's no secret that her death keeps me up. She was my world. Sure, it was awkward at first; I was a few centuries old when me and her married, she was barely nineteen. But we eventually grew to love each other."

Katherine felt Hades squeeze her hand.

"The myth of me kidnapping her is wrong; the marriage was arranged. Her mother, Demeter, thought that the marriage would give Persephone some responsibility. It was hard at first; I was use to having my own way and ruling my kingdom on my own and Persephone had never left earth. But after a while, we got to know each other and became friends."

Hades couldn't help but smile, though he felt pained. He never talked about his feelings about his wife's death, it wasn't normal for him. But with his feelings for Katherine growing, and after tonight, he knew that Katherine deserved to know. He didn't want her to think she was a replacement in the eyes of the servants and nymphs.

"Strangely, we worked well together. She taught me to listen to each soul and guide them through the confusion, especially if they believed in a religion. She often visited some of the souls in their after lives to see how they were; they loved her.

"Over time, I slowly found myself falling in love with her. I was infatuated with everything about her: her smile, her laugh, everything. She was a breath a fresh air. She brought life into the castle. She expanded the garden and helped Hecate take care of the hell-hounds. Cerberus was extremely fond of her. No one really played with him besides me, so he was happy to have a playmate."

"She sounds wonderful."

"Sounded. She died less than five years ago years ago."

"I'm sorry."

"It's alright. At the time, she was unhappy. Even though I told her her life on earth would be completely separate from her life down here, she fell in love with a mortal."

"Who was it?"

Hades shrugged. "I'm not sure. I tried to stay out of her other life. But it was awkward to see him step up while she was here. The moment I saw her look at that man with such love and devastation when he died, I knew.

"She pleaded for me for weeks to bring him back to life, but I'm ruler over the dead; I can only take life, not give it. There, she wanted me to take her life so she could go to the afterlife with him. I absolutely refused.

"When I refused to take her life, she was furious. She moved out of our room and into a separate chamber on the other side of castle. She stopped playing with Cerberus, stopped interacting with the souls. Everyone knew something was wrong; the woman they saw was not the queen they knew."

Katherine's heart began to break. Not just for Hades, but for Persephone. She always believed that you if love two people, you always go to the second person; because if you were really in love with the first, you wouldn't have a second. Katherine couldn't imagine the emotions Hades felt when his own wife asked him to kill her. But Persephone obvisiously loved the human too. She might of loved Hades before, but people do fall out of love.

What made Persephone stop loving Hades?

"After a few years," Hades continued, his hand tightening around Katherines, "I decided to do it. I realized that no matter how much I hated it, Persephone no longer loved me. She might have before, but not then.

"It was hard, seeing her own life draining out of her body. My family, The Counsil, stayed and watch. Demeter was furious with both me and her daughter. She thought I didn't try hard enough and that Persephone was selfish to fall for a mortal. I haven't spoken to her since.

"After her death, my reign over the Underworld started slipping. In today's age, too many people are once; it's overwhelming. My family wants me to find a wife before Persephone's anniversary, or else I fade and someone else takes over."

He looked over at Katherine, his eyes glossy. "It's scary to feel the things I feel now. Before, I felt cold and moved through the days without much consciousness. Now, with you here, I feel things I haven't felt in a long time. You brighten my day with just a simple smile. Everyone adores you, even my family thinks you might save me."

Taking her hand, he brought it to his chest, right over his heart. Katherine blushed with her fingers touched his chest, the coolness tickling the tips of her fingers. She felt his heart beating at a rapid pace, almost like her heart was beating right now; hammering in her ribcage.

"My heart hasn't beat in over ten years years. Since you came, it started beating again. Ever since the ball, I can't get you out of my head. Having you close to me, I felt alive. Sleeping next to you; I finally have peaceful dreams. You do something to me that no one besides Persephone has done."

Hades moved closer to Katherine, his body flushed against hers. Katherine held her breath as she felt his breath against her neck. "I know that I can't get over her in a single night, and you don't deserve to be second to her. But you are not a replaccment to her, and you never will be."

Katherine's heart skipped a few beats. Hades had feelings for her! She had only hoped before that he felt something; now, his words confirmed it.

"I really want to kiss you," he whispered, his voice thick and husky.

Before she could even think, Katherine whispered "Then do it."

Suddenly, she felt his lips against hers.

CHAPTER 19

Everything in Hades' world seemed to stop once his lips met hers. Fireworks exploded behind his eyes, filling his body in blistering colors. Everything seemed to come to life; emotions that were buried deep down in the back of his mind were starting to resurface, coming forth to the front of his mind.

He would be lying if these feelings didn't intimidate him. He hadn't felt like this in centuries. Now, with Katherine, he was tasting, feeling, and seeing everything in bright colors.

He pulled Katherine closer to him, his hands tightening on her waist. He could taste strawberries and mint, a taste that he knew he would grow addicted to.

Katherine never expected for someone she grew to love to be kissing her, to admit his feelings to her. She never had any boy or man to want her; they always wanted Namie. She didn't blame them, Namie was the definition of perfection. But now, here she was, sharing her first kiss with the God of the Underworld.

The voices in her head were full on screaming at her; wails upon wails of curses and insults. The longer she kissed Hades, the more the voices got louder and louder.

Katherine pulled away, clutching her head in agony. The voices felt like someone was stabbing at her head over and over again. Once she had pulled away, the voices and the pain subsided.

Hades held her tightly. He watched as Katherine started to calm down, rubbing her head trying to relieve the pain. He had never seen a spell inflict physical pain on the one the spell was place on. Hecate was nowhere in the castle or even close to it; like she had disappeared.

Hecate kept her distance from the castle, hiding in the shadows. She kept her pressence masked, knowing that Hades was trying to find her. She knew that Hades would ask her to lift the spell, but she couldn't. Apollo threatened her family; he would eventually find out that Hecate lifted the spell, and kill everyone she loved.

She couldn't risk it. It was better to hide and keep her family safe until the month was over.

Unless...

Dissolving her body into black mist, Hecate slivered into the shadows of the cavern and blended into the darkness, in search of the one who might be able to help.

"Are you okay, Katherine," Hades asked, his voice laced with worry.

Katherine nodded. She told him how the voices from the spell made her feel pain, like they were stabbing into her mind until she pulled away from the kiss.

"I've never seen a spell like this," Hades said. "Whatever this spell is, is fueled by jealousy and possession. Whoever casted this spell obviously doesn't want you with me."

Katherine was scared, very scared. She didn't want to be controlled by a spell. She didn't like the idea that someone wanted to manipulate her feelings, to have her has a thing on the self. For the first time in her life, she felt safe and happy that she found someone. Now it was being taken away.

"Do you have any enemies?"

Hades chuckled, though it wasn't humoress. "Too many to count."

"Could it be someone who admired Persephone and feels that I'm replacing her?"

"It's possible. Many souls admired Persephone when she was here, but they aren't powerful to cast such a spell. Most are mere mortals without knowledge of witchcraft. Only Hecate has that much power."

"Could Hecate possibly casted the spell?"

Hades shook his head. "I don't think she would."

If only they knew...

A few days passed by.

No one had seen or heard from Hecate since the night Katherine was possessed, nor have any of the Gods seen Apollo around much besides from a few counsel meetings.

Athena and Hera didn't like how Apollo was behaving these last couple of days. He always had this smirk on his face; like he knew something no one else did. And every time the Counsel was dismissed, Apollo quickly went away to somewhere.

"Something is up with him," Hera told her husband Zeus one day. "It's like he knows something about what's happening to Katherine."

"I've already spoken with him, honey," Zeus cooed at his wife. "He says that he knows nothing about the spell."

"But what about when Athena showed us the..."

"Hera, let's not discuss it right now."

Athena was having no luck either. She was interogating all of the castle staff in the Underworld, asking what happened that night. They all said the same thing: there was a dark, menacing shadow rush to the old music room. They also said that no one saw Hecate afterwards or the days following.

Athena knew that Hecate had something to do with it. She was the Goddess of Witchcraft and the mother of witches. Was it really a coincidence that the same night that Katherine was possessed was the same night that Hecate vanished?

She tried to tell Hades that hecate must've casted the spell, but to no avail. Hades was stressed about Katherine. Her condition was steadily getting worse, and Hades felt he neede to be around her at all times, along with her sister. Hermes and Charos have been sorting the souls and taking them to their afterlives, but they weren't Hades.

Athena saw that Hades was extremely fond of the girl, more than before. Something had chaged inside of him. Whenever she saw him beside Katherine's bed while she slept, he had this look in his eyes; a look that she hadn't seen in him since Persephone.

Truthfully, she never liked Persephone. Although she adored Demeter, her aunt, Persephone seemed different.

She was like a typical nineteen year old during those times. Why Demeter arranged for her young daughter to marry an eons old God of the Dead, Athena didn't know. But after words about Persephone's affair and demands of dying to be with him broke out, something died inside of him.

She cared for her uncle. She didn't like the idea of Persephone being selfish and not consider how her actions affected Hades. But the damage was done.

Now, Hades was different. She saw the old cyrstal throne at the Hallows Eve Ball, and she saw how much that throne suited Katherine, like it was made for her. Hades looked...happy when he and the human shared a dance, how angry he looked when he showed Athena the pictures.

Could Hades have fallen in love with a human?

The thought of that made Athena content. Katherine was making her uncle happy.

Katherine woke up one morning in a cold sweat. Her heart was pounding in her chest and her skin was clammy. Dreams from the night flashed in front of her eyes, images of Apollo and Hades. One moment, it was Hades smiling at her; the next, it was Apollo.

She saw Hades beside her, his head resting on the bed as he sat in a chair he pulled out. His hair was sticking out and ruffled up. He was still alseep.

The voices didn't like Hades being so close to Katherine. They kept screaming and screaming at Katherine to get away from the god all throughout the night, but Katherine liked having Hades with her. She felt safe with him.

Removing the covers, Katherine carefully got out of bed, not wanting to wake Hades. She climbed out of bed and got some fresh clothes before heading into the bathroom.

Hades yawned as he raised his head, his neck and back aching from the uncomfortable position. When he looked at the empty bed, he didn't see Katherine. She must be in the bathroom.

He got up from the chair, stretching his sore limbs. Over the last few nights, Katherine's condition hadn't improve. The spell must be starting to break her down fastly before it continues it's purpose.

Hecate was still missing, which didn't help Hades. Only she knew how to break a spell, especially a spell like this one. Where could she be?

Hades slipped on his shirt before Katherine came out of the bathroom, dressed in a off shoulder sweater and leggings. Some of the marks on her shoulder were now faint and pink instead of the intense red. The bite marks were still there, some even scarring. Apollo must've used a lot of power and strength that night.

Hades wanted to rip Apollo apart so badly. He wanted to send Apollo to Tartarus along with the Titans, far away from Katherine. But if the Counsel didn't even listen to Athena, then why would they listen to him?

Katherine emerged from the bathroom, wearing an off shoulder sweater and leggings. The marks on her skin were finally gone now, but the bite marks were still there, now scarred into the skin. The sight made Hades growl.

Today, Hades had to take care of the dead. For the last few days, Hermes and Charos have been trying to sort the dead. But every day there were more souls to replace the last ones. If Hades didn't help, then the Underworld and the realm above would be in chaos.

He had Namie watch Katherine while he was working. He didn't tell the older sister about the spell; she would accuse him of casting it like when she accused him of raping Katherine.

He walked over to Katherine and hugged her close to him, holding her like she might slip from his grip. He felt her hands tighten as she grabbed his shirt, not wanting him to leave her alone. She didn't like the idea of not having Hades near her, but she knew that the Underworld was in disarray without him.

"I'll be back whenever I can. I promise."

"Alright."

Reluctantly, Hades pulled away before kissing he ron the forehead. A sweet and simple gesture that enraged the voices inside Katherine's head.

Katherine watched as Hades gave her one last smile--it didn't even reach his eyes--before leaving her alone in her room.

Chapter 20

They say that eyes are windows into the soul. By looking into someone's eyes, you can see everything about them: their vices, virtues, goodness, darkness, their past and present. You see it all.

Before, when Hades looked into Katherine's eyes, he saw the pain from hidden wounds, the fear she hid: but he also saw something twinkle behind all that darkness. He didn't realize it at first, but now he realized it was adoration...for him.

Now...her blue eyes were dull, a complete void of nothing. Her eyes were often more black than blue, which scared the god. It would happen when he was too close to her, a mere touch from him now set off the voices in her head.

She would scream from the pain, clutching her head. Hades wanted to comfort her, hold her close, but he couldn't. He had already caused enough damage just being with her. Whoever caused the spell obviously hated Hades and was using Katherine to get to him.

A few weeks had gone by, and Katherine slowly got worse. With her soul weak and vulnerable, the darkness inside her changed its plan. She said it was constantly talking to her to get away from Hades, that she loved someone else. Having her own feelings be manipulated both hurt and angered Hades. Why would someone who was out to get him try to change Katherine's own emotions and thoughts?

There was only a week left in the month before the darkness completes it's job. Hades knew that his sister and neice was trying to find Hecate and whoever casted the spell. Athena believed that Hecate had done something and ran away to avoid justice. Hades didn't believe it.

Hecate would never do such a thing unless she had an absolute reason to. Her family was here in the Underworld in full protection: only someone powerful could threaten or possibly kill them.

Like the past few weeks, Hades left his duties to Hermes and Charos. When Hermes was busy, some of the minor gods in the Underworld helped to relieve their God of the Dead. Servants and nymphs stayed clear of the human and god, in fear of being possessed.

Namie helped as best she could. When Katherine would go into a "fit," Namie was there to calm her down. Sometimes it helped, other times not. If it was one if those days that it didn't, both her and Hades watched the one they loved suffer.

Right now, Namie was with Katherine to keep an eye on her. Hades sat in the garden, near Katherine's favorite flower.

Ironically, she had no idea that that flower was Persephone's flower, one she personally planted.

That flower reminded Hades of the love he lost. Persephone brought so much joy, but she was so naive when it came to both love and being a goddess. Sure, she could make plants grow for a short time and interact with the souls, but she was so young. She was only nineteen, both in human and god.

Persephone never experienced hardship or pain. Katherine did. Katherine grew in her sisters shadow and broke when she saw the one person who loved her killed. Her parents abandoned her to deal with their own problems.

In many ways, Katherine was like Hades. In many ways.

Hades ran his hand through his hair, tugging it out of frustration.

It was his fault that Katherine was like this. If he had never brought her here, she would still be up in the world above.

He remembered back to that day, that day in the park.

It was raining, he remembered. The sky was gray and bleak, the wind cold. Hades rode in the sky above, invisible to the mortal eye. It was rare for him to be up on earth; he normally stayed out of Zeus' and Posideon's domain. But he was curious about something.

One of the souls, Namie was her name, had regained her memories and was in a panic about her younger sister Katherine. She begged and begged for the god to just check on her to see if she was safe. Hades refused: why would he go see if a mere human hadn't killed herself yet?

But nonetheless, if it kept the soul from pestering him, he agreed.

So here he was, flying over the city in search of the sister.

It wasn't hard to find her. The darkness that surrounded that girl, anyone could sense it. Hades could feel the sadness and pain from the girl. It was thick and heavy, clinging to the gray sky as if the bleakness was its last drop of water.

On some level, Hades saw himself in that girl's soul. According to the older sister, Katherine Bakers was known to be depressed due to her classmates bullying her or her parents never giving her the attention she needed. He could tell by the sister, Namie was Katherine's only friend and who cared.

Almost like how Persephone-at first-was the only who Hades had...

He shook his head. Persephone was dead. He would, soon too, fade out of his existence. Just a few more years.

Hades saw the young girl. She was sitting under a dead tree, ablivious to the world around her. She looked like she was crying, her body shaking as she sobbed, almost making the god pity her... Almost.

Hades spoke to the horses in a determined tone with his native tongue and pulled the chariot to the ground, still invisible to any human.

As he started to land, he saw that there was someone dressed in black standing behind Katherine. Instead of the depression that seemed to roll off her effortlessly, he sensed such an intense fear come from her, it nearly surprised him.

That man... Is that Namie Bakers murderer?

The man was holding a gun close to her back, yet Katherine never moved. It was as if she knew she was about to die and was content with it. The man raised the gun and hit Katherine in the head. Hades watched as Katherine fell to the ground unconscious. Hades could sense the satisfaction from the killer. He knew that if he didn't at least scare the man away, gods only know what he might do to her.

Making himself visible, Hades landes the chariot, the horses neaing and hitting the ground with their powerful hooves. It was enough to spook the man because he abandoned whatever plan he had and left.

Katherine laid on the cold ground, her clothes soaked. She wore a baggy hoodie and black pants, her long dark hair caked in mud.

He jumped out of the chariot and walked over to the girl. Up close, he observed that she looked attractive for a human. Though her and Namie looked very similar, almost like twins despite the age gap, Katherine looked...familiar. Her pale olive skin, small petite frame... She looked almost like...

Nonsense, Hades thought. There was no way this girl looked like his dead wife.

Picking her up bridal style, Hades gently placed her into the chariot and rode off to the Underworld.

Hades chuckled at the memory. Who knew that a lot would change since then. It felt like an eternity since they day. The god had fallen in love with a human.

Suddenly, a loud and blood curdling scream rang through the cavern. Any nymph in the garden stopped dead cold at the scream. Hades rushed into the castle to Katherine's room.

Kicking the doors open, Hades saw Katherine on the floor, screaming with Namie a little ways away, shaken with fear. Hades could see that Katherine's eyes were pitch black with no light in them.

Hades rushed to her side, not touching her even though he was itching to comfort her. Her screams rung in his ears, burning themselves into his memory. His heart broke as Katherine laud there, twisting and turning as if something was moving inside her.

He had never seen a possession like this. Who was doing this? If they wanted him, why did they target Katherine?

Hades hated himself in that moment. The one time since Persephone, the one moment that he thought he could love again, someone had took that away from him.

After a while, Katherine calmed down enough for Hades to carry her to her bed. Her body was scorching hot, sweat beading down her forehead. Hades laid her down the bed, not bothering to cover her up in the blankets.

How could something bring a mighty god, one of the first gods since the creation of him and his brothers and sisters, be brought to his knees?

Hades kissed her forehead, his lips tasting the salt on her forehead, and left without a word.

CHAPTER 21

Hecate came to the small cottage at the end of the forest. The sun was bright in the sky, the illusion almost fooling Hecate. It was her idea to give each afterlife a realistic look.

The air was thick with the smell of flowers and pollen. There was a faint sound of chirping of birds, the sounds of insects singing their songs. The grass was a bright green under the sun.

The cottage was big enough for just two, nothing more. The roof and walls were covered in green vines, tiny flowers blossoming in different colors.

Shifting to her physical form, Hecate walked up the cobblestone path to the cottage of the former Queen of the Underworld.

It had been years since Heacte saw the naive goddess. She never really liked the queen, just because she felt that Persephone was too young and immature to rule over millions of souls. But Hades was happy to have someone, so it wasn't in Hecate's place to complain.

Taking a deep breath, she knocked on the old wooden door, praying that Persephone could help. This seemed like a good idea considering--

The door opened a girl stepped out. Her long dark hair was in a high ponytail, a bandana tied around her head. Her long pink dress was littered with dirt as if she just got done planting a garden.

She looked the exact same as the day she died. No wonder others from the castle said Katherine looked like the late goddess.

"Hecate?" Persephone asked, her brows furrowed in confusion as to why a goddess of witchcraft was at her cottage. "What are you doing here?"

"I need your help. Something bad is happening, and I think you are the only one who might be able to do something."

"If you're asking power wise, they disappeared once I died. I'm useless."

Hecate shook her head. "No, you're not. I think you really can help. Just at least hear me out; if you can't help, then you might know someone who can."

"Alright, come on in. Adonis won't be back until nightfall."

Persephone stepped aside and opened the door wider. Hecate walked in as Persephone closed the door. The ceiling and banisters were wrapped in vines: leaves, flowers, and fruits hanging off. It was stuffy with all the smells from the flowers; it made Hecate light-headed.

The goddesses took a seat in a few worn chairs near the fireplace. It was always warm, there was no need for a fire.

"So, why are you here? Does it involve Hades?"

"No, it's a human."

"A mortal? In the Underworld?"

"Yes. Her name is Katherine Bakers. Hades brought her here a little over a month ago, before Hallows Eve. She has a sister here who was killed when she was fourteen."

Persephone tsked. "Poor girl."

Hecate nodded. "Something happened after the Hallows Eve Ball... Apollo has been obsessed with her since. He came to me and made me cast a spell on her to make her fall for him instead of Hades. He threatened my family; my husband and children. Afterwards, I ran. And now I'm here."

Persephone pursed her lips, her burrows furrowed in thought. "How does the spell work?"

"The spell is more of a physical form. It first starts as voices to break down that individual. Then it spell will start expanding to the body; and finally, the voices start to convince that person of whatever the caster wants them to believe... In this case, Apollo wants Katherine to love him instead of Hades. The voices will try to convince her weaken soul to give in."

"How long will the spell last?"

"I had it take place in a month. Right now, it would be in the final stage; convincing her."

They were silent for a moment. Besides Apollo, no one knew about the terrible thing Hecate did to Katherine. Now a former goddess knows.

"What does this girl mean to Hades?"

"Why do you ask?"

Persephone shrugged. "I was wondering if he ever found someone after what happened. After what I did, he needs someone to help with the Underworld and to mend the damages I caused."

Hecate nodded. "He cares for her, deeply. Everyone can see it. He even kissed her. I suspect it could've been more if it wasn't for the spell. The spell causes physical pain to the person if the object of the rejection is near. So when Hades touches her or is near her, she experiences pain.

"I have no ill-will to the girl. She clearly does make Lord Hades happy... But my family..."

Persephone nodded, her face blank, not showing the range of emotions raging inside her mind. Everything from content to firey rage boiling her blood.

She knew very well how Apollo was; he was a sadistic monster.

During her time in the mortal world, she and Apollo spent a lot of time together. She had freedom there I the world above, so why not see where they went.

He was nice at first. They would talk all through the night about anything that was on their mind. He was so charming, caring, and sweet. He taught her archery and the ways of poetry. He was perfect.

When they both admitted their growing feelings a few summers after, Persephone thought it would all be perfect.

But it wasn't...

She saw a side of Apollo that she never saw. It was like a 360. He went from sweet and caring to dark and controlling.

When she would go back to the Underworld, Apollo would sneak into her chamber and do god awful things to her. It was easy to hide the bites and bruises, but it took a toll.

The only reason why Apollo stopped was because of Adonis was in that field. If it wasn't for him, Persephone would've had the same or worse fate as Katherine Bakers.

"How can I help the girl? I have no powers anymore."

"I have a theory..."

Adonis came home long after Hecate left. He stepped through the door to see his beloved pacing the floor, her hair a mess from the numerous times she ran her hand through it. The look of stress was evident on her face.

"Kore?"

"Adonis. Something bad has happened. Something really bad."

Adonis rushed to his beloved, his mind racing with anything that could go wrong. "What is it?"

"Remember when I told you back when, that I was constantly sick and feeling pain in my abdominal?"

Adonis looked at the former goddess in fear and confusion. "You don't mean..."

Persephone nodded. "And because of it, I just put a mortal's life in danger."

CHAPTER 22

Hades sat on his throne, the grand room dark. The souls were gone, the chaos quiet; everything was silent.

He felt so tired and exhausted. The month was nearly over...just a few days. Katherine was barely hanging on. He could tell she was slipping fast, but what could he do to help? It was his fault that she was like this.

It was no longer a mystery that the one behind it was Apollo. Hades heard Katherine scream his name one night while she tried to sleep. Just, why? What was about Katherine that Apollo wanted? She was a mere mortal after all. She had no powers, nothing special to attract the attention of a sadistic god like Apollo.

He was always power-hungry; so what was it about Katherine that attracted his unwanted attention?

Though Hades rarely dealt with the Oracle of Delphi, she had to know of something as to why Apollo done this. But she was his oracle, would she even tell Hades behind his god's back? If she did ever betray her god, Apollo would surely kill her and replace her.

He ran his hand through his hair, letting out a frustrated groan.

If Persephone was here...

No, he couldn't think like that. That path led to only hurt and grief. He already messed up by calling Katherine Persephone that night long ago. The guilt still ate at him. He was so angry and disappointed in himself. If Katherine survives this, she would never be with him.

Getting up from the throne, Hades walked out of the throne room and out to the garden. The gem flowers glistened in the limited light, the fountain still gushing out water in the center of the maze. Hades hummed as he walked to the center of the garden.

A part of him wanted to see Persephone's flowers one last time before he got rid of them. Even though Katherine had an attachment for these flowers, they reminded him of Persephone. He didn't want a constant reminder when there was already a girl that he was growing closer and closer.

His mind still buzzed at the thought of their kiss. She tasted sweet like freshly picked strawberries and mint. The taste was addicting. He didn't want to stop.

His heart was hammering in his chest, feeling the weight in his chest begin to lift. But that weight soon reappeared once Katherine began to pull back in pain.

Something inside him shattered. He hadn't felt that much pain since Persephone's passing.

Were the Fates so against him finding peace and happiness?

He came to the patch of Persephone's flowers. The midnight gem glistened with tiny specks of colors in the dim light. Their edges were smooth yet jagged on some petals.

"I hope you're not mad," Persephone said as she held out a black gemmed flower, a rainbow of colors exploding in the light.

Hades never expected for a goddess who was so bright to create a dark and mysterious gem.

She always seemed to amaze him.

Taking the flower out of her palm, Hades kneeled down to an open spot near the center fountain and with a flick of his wrist, the flower became one with the cavern dirt.

"There. Only thing left is to create more."

That was one of times Hades truly saw Persephone smile.

Hades sat on his knees, his hand near the flower. His chest felt heavy as all their memories together flooded his mind. Ghosts of the past.

Grabbing a fist full of the flower, Hades crushed it into dust. The other similar flowers soon turned to dust, leaving an empty spot behind.

His cheeks felt cool from the tears that managed to fall, dropping onto his lap. A small part of the weight on his chest lifted as the dust settled.

Hades began to think about a new flower to put there. Even if Katherine wanted nothing to do with him after this, he still wanted to a part of her to remain when he faded.

He imagined a large rose with jagged edges in the petals. It would be black as night in the dark, but in the light, it would turn white with every color when hit at any angle. He normally stayed away from the color white, but to him, it suited Katherine.

With the image in his head, Hades whispered in his native tongue as the image began to glow bright in his mind, before the light dimmed and the image was gone. Opening his eyes, he saw the jeweled rose in his palm.

It was enormous. One petal was about six inches long. The flower would easily fit the empty place. He placed the flower down and like before, the cavern bent at his will, rooting the flower there to stay forever.

Standing up, Hades felt proud of the flower. No one besides him could destroy it, not like he wanted to destroy it. It was Katherine's flower.

"I always wondered when you would destroy my flower."

Everything in Hades' body froze at her voice. A voice he hadn't heard in years.

Persephone.

Was.

There.

Right there, behind him.

Slowly, Hades turned around to see her.

She looked the same as she did when she died; even the same dress. She looked so much like Katherine...

"Persephone?" Hades questioned, not believing his eyes.

"It's me," she smiled, though it looked sad. "I never thought I would be back here. Hecate didn't lie when she said everything looked the same."

"Hecate? She was with you?" Hecate was with his dead wife the whole time?

"She had some...trouble here and thought I might help. She really dug herself a hole with him."

"Trouble? You mean... She was the one to cast the spell on Katherine?"

It was hard to not chuckle at Hades. It was evident that he cares about that human girl. All Persephone wanted was to have her husband find someone new. Hecate spike on how their relationship was starting to grow; he even kissed the girl for gods sake.

Hades was never one to vocalize his feelings. It was nice to see him finally overcome their past together.

Persephone nodded. "Apollo blackmailed her to doing the spell. She said that he found her family here in the Underworld and threatened to kill her family and her."

It made sense, Hades thought. That's why she wasn't here: she went to go look for Persephone. But... Why Persephone?

Before Hades could even ask her why she was here, a loud and blood curdling scream came from the balcony above. Katherine's room.

Hades didn't hesitate to jump up to the balcony, not bothering to look to see if Persephone was behind him. Peering through the curtains, he saw Katherine limp and unconscious in the arms of Apollo.

Chapter 23

Before Hades could even ask her why she was here, a loud and blood curdling scream came from the balcony above. Katherine's room.

Hades didn't hesitate to jump up to the balcony, not bothering to look to see if Persephone was behind him. Peering through the curtains, he saw Katherine limb and unconscious in the arms of Apollo.

Apollo had that malicious and victorious gleam in his eyes as he held the unconscious girl close to him.

He knew what this girl was. The Oracle of Delphi told him about this mortal girl and what she could do if she ever found out who she truly was.

With the spell nearly completed, she would be his before morning.

"Apollo!"

Apollo looked to see the enraged god at the balcony. For a split moment, Apollo looked at Hades in fear, but it was gone in a flash before his attention turned back to Katherine.

"Let her go," Hades sneered. He felt close to the edge, an edge that could cause damage to the world above. The only thing he wanted was for Apollo to get his hands off the woman he loves.

Loves...

I love Katherine. I always have.

Not now, he bit at himself. That will have to wait.

Stepping further into the room, Hades could see that Katherine was close to falling off the edge. Though she was unconscious, her eyes were open, black and soulless, starring out into nothingness. Her skin was sickly pale and looked icy cold. The darkness inside her was starting to show up on her skin, faint black swirls on her body.

"I guess that bitch behind you told you everything?" Apollo sneered, his heart squeezing at the sight of his old love.

Persephone stepped from behind Hades, her eyes bright with anger. Despite her tiny size, Apollo knew she was one to not test. Even though she had no powers, she was still a goddess.

Apollo loved her.

She was his everything.

All those times when she came to earth and they met in the fields. Before that damned human took her from him.

He loved her.

But he couldn't have her. And if he couldn't have her, the next best thing was... Katherine.

"Let her go, Apollo," Persephone commanded. "You of all people know what that girl is capable of. All because of your Oracle."

Apollo laughed. "Of course I know. Why do you think I want her? She can be what helps me take over Mount Olympus. Zeus isn't fit to rule."

"And you are," Hades asked. "Everyone knows how corrupt you are! You are a power-hungry god who wants my brother's throne."

"I don't want the throne. Being the new Father of the Gods means having control over everything...even death itself."

Apollo looked at Persephone, and for once, he didn't bother hiding what he felt. "I loved you, Kore. You left me in both life and death."

"You never loved me. You were controlling and forced me to do things I never wanted. Adonis saved me that day in the field. I will love him more than I did with you. I was blind to see it."

Apoll shook his head. "It doesn't matter now. I have Katherine. She can easily replace you. Once she wakes up, she'll be mine. So if you want to say your goodbyes, dear uncle, say them now."

"You're. Not. Taking. Her."

The air in the room shifted. Everything seemed darker, unstable. Like the ground after an earthquake. Persephone stepped back from the angry god, knowing what he was going to do.

In a flash, the two gods were engulfed into darkness.

The Shadow Realm.

Apollo looked around in the pitch blackness, trying to find Hades. He should've known Hades would do something like this. He's the most powerful in the Shadow Realm.

He looked down to see Katherine gone. Humans couldn't enter the Shadow Realm.

But she's not human.

Katherine felt cold. She felt tired and sore. All she wanted to do was let go and sleep.

She was so weak from trying to fight off the darkness. But it was too powerful, too dark.

It felt like years since she saw light. Something other than darkness. The voices were gone, already done with their job.

She no longer saw Hades in her mind. It was only Apollo.

Maybe it was best to let go. The spell was complete. There was nothing to help her.

"Katherine."

A voice echoed in the darkness. It sounded so faint and distant. Katherine thought it was just another voice from before.

"Katherine."

The voice sounded a little louder, but it sounded so far away.

"Katherine. Please, answer me. We can help you."

Nothing can help me...

"Yes, we can."

Suddenly, a small light pierced through the darkness. The harsh light blinded Katherine, burning her eyes. Katherine hissed at the light.

The light dimmed down, and there, in the darkness, stood two girls. One looked like a typical Gothic girl, and the other...looked exactly like her.

Persephone?

The girl–Persephone–chuckled. Her soft laugh felt warm and inviting. "Yes dear, I'm Persephone. Me and Hecate are here to help you come home."

Home?

"Yes. With Hades, where you belong."

Hades?

Both goddesses nodded before walking through the darkness towards Katherine.

Home. Katherine hadn't felt at home since Namie's death. Her old house felt cold and empty.

When she came to the Underworld, it felt cold and dark. Hades wasn't really welcoming to her at first, but it was all a facade. He was a broken man who was hurting over the death of his wife, a wife who told him to kill her so she could be with a mortal man.

Katherine never thought that a man like him would ever have the same feelings for her. But that kiss... She thought it was out of pity, but it wasn't. It proved that he was ready to move on...with her.

Persephone being here proved it. She looked happy to see Katherine. There was a gleam of hope in her eyes. She too wanted her husband to move on.

The two goddesses kneeled down closer to Katherine. Hecate was whispering in a foreign language, her palms out. There was a soft glow radiating from her hands.

Persephone smiled down at Katherine, stroking her hair softly. "You was right, Hecate. Seeing her only proved it."

Proved what?

"Don't worry, I'll tell you."

Apollo gripped his side, his hand warm from the blood. His powers were weak from the fight and from the darkness. The Shadow Realm paralyzed his abilities as long as Hades kept him here.

If he didn't escape, Hades will kill him.

No god besides the three brothers could kill another god. Hades was the deadliest out of the three. He could send his soul to the deepest and darkest place in Tartarus...where the Titans are.

No god could survive there.

Quickly healing the open gash in his side, Apollo took out his sword, prepared to fight.

"Why do you even want Katherine," Apollo yelled into the darkness. "You don't even know what she is. Besides, why would she want you? You're still hung over for Persephone!"

The shadows shreaked and rumbled. Apollo covered his ears, cursing at the shadows. Damn shadows.

The shadows shreaked for a moment longer before dying down. The God uncovered his ears, relieved that they stopped.

"You want me to tell you what Katherine is? She's a descendent of Persephone. Persephone had a mortal child with that idiot human Adonis, and that child grew up to have another child, and so on. The Oracle told me that there would be human who was a descendent of the late goddess who would inheraite great powers. She could easily tip the balance if needed.

"Besides, it's too late anyways. She's gone. She's mine now, so why bother fighting?"

There was only silence. The darkness quivered as it slowly retreated back. Light began to fill the bedroom chamber.

Hades stood near the bed, silent as he wisked the Shadow Realm away. He looked battered, the few wounds on his body healing quickly.

Persephone was gone, but Katherine now laid limp on the floor near Apollo. Her eyes were now closed, like she was asleep.

Apollo looked at Hades before smirking and picking up the unconscious girl.

"Any last words?"

"I do."

Both gods looked at Katherine, shocked to see her awake. She still looked pale, but the color was coming back to her cheeks.

Hades couldn't pinpoint it, but she seemed different. Her soul felt different. There was no darkness in her soul. Where did it go?

Katherine placed her hand on Apollo's bare chest. Apollo hissed when her hand touched his skin. It was hot and burning.

He quickly dropped her, confused as to why she burned him. The spell... What happened?

Persephone and Hecate appeared. Hecate looked drained of energy, Persephone was the only one holding her up. She looked at Katherine and nodded her head, like they both agreed to something.

Katherine nodded in understanding and walked over to Apollo.

The energy in the room shifted. Everyone felt it. Apollo gulped in fear, knowing what this girl was now. Her true soul was awake.

"How did..."

"QUIET!"

The room shuddered at her voice. The power in her voice almost made Hades quiver.

If Apollo wasn't afraid before, he was now.

"Now..." Katherine said calmly. "I want you leave my home. Your family will see what is just for you. If you so much as step one foot in the Underworld, I will personally send you to Tartarus. Do. You. Understand?"

Apollo nodded. He stood up, and in a flash, he was gone.

Katherine got up and looked over at the goddesses and the god she loved.

"Katherine?"

Tears filled her eyes when she looked at Hades. She saw every emotion in his eyes, it was nearly overwhelming.

"Hades."

The sound of her voice. It sounded like her, but yet, it didn't. She looked the same, but she didn't.

Where is the girl he loved?

CHAPTER 24

I t had been a few days since Katherine woke up as...what ever she was now. She felt different, lighter and stronger. Any shred of darkness inside had vanished. Well, except the gaping hole still in her heart.

She must've had some realistic idea on how Hades would react. If she was...normal, she imagined him hugging her and kissing her. But he didn't. He just stared at her before walking out of the room, mumbling "She's not the same."

He was right. Katherine was different.

She was a descendant of Persephone, the former goddess of the Underworld. A descendant of the Greek gods that she believed to only be tales.

Persephone explained to her that she didn't realize that the child she had would ever survive. "Times were different then," she said. "Girls were subjected to so much at such an early age. I never told Adonis about his daughter. Of course he knew something was wrong when I was sick, but I hid my belly by some illusions Iris gave to me."

"What about my sister, Namie?"

"She didn't inherent my line. She's purely human."

"So, what does that make me?"

"Well, in most cases, you would be a demigod, a hero of the gods. But you're not my direct child. My child never showed strength or abilities, so I never thought of it, aside from the fact I never expected for them to survive long enough to have children. I believe you're merely a reincarnation of part of my being."

Katherine looked at the goddess in confusion. "I thought reincarnation was a soul transfering to another body?"

Persephone nodded. "It is, for humans. It's rare for part of a god to have a part of them in someone else. But I was with a mortal man in the human world, not with Hades. So you are still human, but you do possess the powers of a god."

Despite Persephone's patience to explain it, Katherine was still confused. She wasn't a god, but possessed god-like abilites.

For the last few days, she spent her time in the maze, away from everyone. Namie would come out from time to time, trying to comfort her, but Katherine wanted to be left alone. Cerberus, the little puppy that Hades showed her during the early days of her stay, sat near her feet, doing the only thing a normal dog would do.

He didn't beg for attention. He didn't try to do anything cute. He was smart enough to know Katherine's mood wouldn't change. So he sat by her feet, providing a silent comfort that she desperately needed.

Who knew the guardian of the Gates to the Underworld would be so considerate.

Katherine sighed before looking up at the castle. From here, she could see the balcony to Hades' chamber. The French doors were closed and the curtains drawned.

Hades hadn't come out of his room since she woke up.

He couldn't even look her in the eye.

"She's not the same."

That hurt Katherine more than anything.

Everything that she felt for him, the memory of him proclaiming his feelings, their kiss...

All of it seemed to slip away from her grasp, turning as thin as sand through a hourglass.

It was stupid for her to think that anything would be the same after she woke up. After all, she wasn't completely human anymore.

Why would Hades want to be with someone who was a decendent between the wife he loved and a mortal?

Maybe it was best that Katherine left the Underworld.

Now that everything about her was out, the souls would be begging her to stay and be their new queen. But she couldn't do that. She wasn't fit to be here anymore, let alone be a queen.

Besides, Persephone was still here. Hades will take her back, keep her here until he fades away. He would want her to be there in his final moments.

Katherine looked down at Cerberus.

He looked up at her, already knowing her train of throught. He whimpered and stood up on his hind legs. Katherine smiled, though it was sad, picked up the puppy and held him close.

"It's okay," Katherine cooed. "It's for the best. Hades doesn't need me anymore. I was a burden from the start; there's no need for me to stay."

Cerberus barked. One of his heads was whimpering and crying. Katherine felt her heart break at the sight.

She hugged him tightly, being careful to not drop him and she stood up and carried him with her back to her room. She didn't want to be alone while she said goodye to her sister.

When she reached her room, she saw Namie sitting on the bed, a somber look on her face.

"You're leaving, aren't you?"

Katherine nodded. "Even if I wanted to stay, Hades won't even look at me anymore. Like he said, I'm not the same anymore. Why would he want someone like me constantly reminding him of his wife who he still loves?"

"He doesn't love her."

"Then why is she still in the palace? He's probably begging her stay with him."

"You can't honestly think that."

"He called me 'Persephone' the night I was possessed by that spell before running off and leaving me alone. Sure, he admitted to having feelings for me and even kissed me, but he'll always love her. I can't be her shadow. I can't be her replacement no matter how hard I try. It's best if I go."

"Do you really feel that?"

Katherine turned around to see a somber looking Hades. His black hair was messy, dark circled under his dark eyes.

Namie picked up the puppy before hurrying out of the room, leaving the two of them alone.

She averted her gaze from his, her heart pounding painfully in her chest.

"Well?"

Katherine didn't say anything, afraid that her vouce would fail her. She didn't expect to see him. She had surely thought he was with Persephone up in his room.

Why does he look like he hasn't sleep in days?

Hades stepped closer, causing Katherine to take a step back. Watching her step away from him made Hades feel angry and irritable.

Was she really going to leave?

Katherine panicked when her back hit a wall, the coolness causing goosebumps to form on her skin. She hadn't felt this scared since the first time they met. She knew that Hades was angry. She didn't tell him that she was leaving. But why should she?

"I'll ask again," he said, his voice low. "Do you really think that way?"

Katherine nodded. "You still love her; it was obvious when you called her name, when she was here to help me. If I wanted to stay, you would only see me as her replacement. Besides, I will only be a reminder of everything she did to you."

"Just because you are a decedent of hers doesn't make you her. She made her choice to be with a mortal man, there's nothing that can be done. But her choices are not reflections of you. I meant it when I said I cared about you. Every time I thought about you, it felt right. My feelings for you grew and grew, even when I didn't want to admit to myself."

The next three words shocked Katherine.

"I love you."

Those three words.

Words that everyone took for granted.

Words that was overused in everything.

It was those three words that Katherine wished to hear all her life. No one truly loved her, not even Namie's sisterly love could fill the void inside her heart. No one wanted to deal with a girl who was depressed and in despair for most of her life, hiding away from the world, finding comfort in music and dance.

She hid in the dark shadows of her mind. At least until she met Hades.

Now, he said the three words that meant everything to her.

"I love you, Katherine. Maybe The Fates wanted us to find each other, or maybe it by sere luck, but my feelings for you aren't changing. I can't imagine you not in my life anymore. I love you."

Katherine's heart was pounding wildly, wanting to burst from all the emotions that were causing havoc in her mind.

"You don't have to say it back," Hades said, feeling worried that Katherine wuld reject him. "I won't keep you from leaving, it's your choice, and I won't keep you here if you don't--"

"I love you too."

"You do?"

Katherine nodded, a smile tugging in her tear stained cheeks. "I always have. I don't know if it's fate or destiny, but I know that you're the one that I've been looking for."

Hades didn't hesitate to kiss Katherine. He held her close to him, not wanting to let her go. She kissed him back just as passionately, clinging to him as her legs felt like jello. She felt like she was on cloud nine, high off this feeling inside of her.

Unlike the first time he kissed her, there was no voices, no pain. Now, it was only bliss.

They soon pulled away, still looking at each other. Katherine still felt her lips tingle from the kiss. Her legs felt weak, and if it wasn't for Hades holding her, she would've fell to the floor.

"How could I leave you now?"

"You're staying?"

Katherine nodded. "I'm staying."

CHAPTER 25

Two months later...

To say that Katherine was nervous was an understatement.

Today was Apollo's trial in front of The Counsel. The Counsel consisted of the original six gods and goddesses who defeated Cronus and the others that followed.

Because the attacks were held in the Underworld, everyone thought was best to hold the trials on earth. It was mutual ground for the Olympic gods and Hades. And because the case was so close to home for both Hades and Katherine, Hades would be sitting out from The Counsel. He had already seen the evidence and his feelings for the human would cloud his already bias verdict.

Everyone was seated in the Parthenon. Satyrs, nymphs, centaurs, and other numerous creatures from Olympus came to see the Sun God's trial. To say that the news shocked them was an understatement.

What was even more shocking was that the Oracle of Delphi knew that all of it was going to happen. She knew about her god's intentions with that human girl and the lengths he was going to go through to overthrow Zeus to resurrect Persephone. That was beyond treason... That was banishment to Tartarus.

Katherine sat inbetween Hades and Hecate, near The Counsel. There was no one in the black throne near the opposite end: Hades' throne. It looked like the throne back in the Underworld. It was towering, the black marble glistening in the sunlight peering into the Parthenon.

She wondered why his throne wasn't with his brothers, Zeus and Posideon. They were the most powerful out of the gods, creators of Olympus, the sea, and the Underworld.

It didn't seem to bother Hades, he was use to being left out in most decisions regarding his family. If it didn't effect the Underworld, it didn't effect him.

But this trial did effect him.

Apollo blackmailed a goddess into manipluating them to help him overthrow the Father of the Gods and mortals. He did everything in the Underworld. It was Hades' business.

But because of his closeness to Katherine, his family saw it was an obsticale to a complete unbias trial.

If it had to be, so be it. Besides, his family wouldn't be able to control him once he saw his nephew.

The only reason he was here was to be there for Katherine. Namie wanted to come, but souls weren't permitted to return to the world of the living. Even a god has to abade to the rules set by The Fates.

Everyone hushed when they saw Apollo, tired and exhausted in his chains, which were constricting his abilites. His usually tan and bright skin seemed dull and almost pale like a mortal's. Everyone seemed to hold their breaths as Apollo walked infront of the platform where the gods and goddesses sat on their thrones.

You could see the hint of nervousness and fear in his eyes once he stood there in his place.

There was no one to defend him. He admitted to everything, so why bother having someone to defend him?

The crowd settled down, waiting for the scene to unfold.

Katherine froze when Apollo looked at her. Though she hated the god for what he put her through, he looked...broken. He didn't look like the god he was before, he looked so tired like he hadn't slept in months. The chains on his wrists were digging into his skin, leaving brusies and lines of dried blood behind.

The longer she looked at him, the more her anger and resentment began to fade away. Maybe she pitied him?

Hades saw Apollo's gaze fall on Katherine, and with a sinister look, Apollo quckly turned away.

"My son," Zeus said, his voice booming in the Parthenon. "Apollo of Delos... You have been charged of treason against the Gods of Olympus, performings sexual acts without consent, and the blackmail of a minor goddess into the manipulation of the human in question, Katherine Bakers. Does this sound correct?"

"Yes," Apollo said, his voice weak.

"When the Counsel decides your fate, it will immediately take affect, and defiance to our decision will result in your existence will fade into nothing. Do you understand?"

"Yes."

"Very well. Let The Counsel begin their verdicts."

A goddess on the far left who sat on a pearl and sea foam throne with roses and swans, who turned out to be Aphrodite, stood from her throne. In the light, she seemed to glow with a beautiful radiants. No wonder she was the goddess of beauty.

Aphrodite stepped forward. "Tartarus," she said in a calm and elegant voice. Apollo nodded, accepting her verdict, before sitting back down on her throne.

The god beside her, a brawny man covered in oil and sweat, stood from his iron and copper throne. He must be Hephaestus, Aphrodite's husband. "Tartarus."

Once again, Apollo nods and accepts his fate.

Katherine sat there in silence as gods and goddesses one by one, each verict the same for all of them.

Fianlly, Hera stood from her throne, larger than the others. She looked so graceful and elegant, a motherly elegance. Like the others, she too gave the same verdict before sitting down beside her husband.

Zeus at last stands up.

"The Counsel has decided. You are to be banished to Tartarus with the other fallen gods and Titans. Hades will decide what to do afterwards."

Any life that was in Apollo seemed to escape his body as the gods disappeared one by one back to Mount Olympus.

The mythical creatures soon begin to leave, murmuring to themselves.

What will become of the Sun God?

Apollo stood there, all alone, looking broken and fragile. Something stirred in Katherine's heart the longer she stared at the god.

"Come on Katherine," Hades said, his voice strained once he followed Katherine's gaze.

He could tell by the look on her face that she was sorry for his nephew, now former god. Words couldn't begun to express how much he was happy to give Apollo everything he deserved for harming Katherine.

But he knew her. It didn't matter to her. She never hated Apollo. Feared, yes. But never hated. Most would hate whoever brought them pain, but not Katherine.

She looked at him, and by the look in her eyes, he knew what she was asking.

Why.

Why he did everything.

It was closure for her. To move forward.

Even though he didn't like the idea of the woman he loved being close to Apollo, he knew that Katherine needed this.

"I'll be here."

She beamed brightly, giving him a peck on the cheek before making her way towards Apollo.

He didn't seem to notice her. He had a distant and shattering look to his face. When he finally acknowledged her, he had a heart shattering look on his face.

"I loved her," he whispered. "I loved her. I may not have been great for her, but I did love her. We were close before she left, and she passed on, it was hard. When the Oracle told me of a descendent of hers, a mortal girl who could change everything, I knew I had to have you. I never really wanted to rule over Olympus, I just wanted the power to...bring her back."

"She's gone," Katherine said. "She's with Adonis in her afterlife. No god could've brought her back, not even I nor Hades. What you did to me..." Katherine cleared her throat, "Is something I could never escape, not even in sleep. So I won't forgive you for that. But, I forgive you for everything else."

Apollo looked at her, eyes clouded in confusion. "You forgive me...?"

Katherine nodded. "I understand. You loved her—even if you didn't show it in the best of ways—and you would've done anything to have her, even if it meant taking me away from the man I love."

"Thank you." Katherine smiled weakly, a weight lifting off her chest. She soon felt an arm wrap around her waist, she didn't have to know who it was.

Hades had a blank face as he stared at his nephew. "Just because she forgives doesn't mean I do. Do not expect me to take your punishment lightly." Apollo nodded.

Hades raised his hand and with a snap of his fingers, Apollo was gone. Gone to Tartarus.

Katherine starred at the spot he was moments ago, the heaviness in her chest leaving her. This was the reason she came to his trial.

She needed to tell him she forgave him.

She looked at Hades, a smile tugging on her lips and a few tears steaming down her face. "Let's go home."

CHAPTER 26

S ix months later...

Hades paced and paced in the throne room up in Olympus, running his fingers through his hair. Anxiety ran through him like Styx. He was never anxious. He was always calm and collected. Yet here he was, pacing his brother's throne room having an anxiety attack.

For the last few weeks, he had been quiet and secretive to Katherine, avoiding her like the plague. He knew that he was hurting her by doing so, but this was important.

This had the Underworld and his existence riding on how he did this.

It felt like an eternity before Zeus and Posideon showed up. Zeus was dressed in a white suit with a golden robe on his shoulders, and Posideon wore a dark navy blue suit with sea green accents, his trident at his side.

Zeus had that knowing smirk on his face when he saw his brother await anxiously for them. Everyone knew that Hades had feeligs for that human girl since she had arrived. Zeus knew why Hades kept his emotions locked up until he was a man of ice, but he also knew Katherine would help thaw him out once again.

"My my, brother," Posideon said. "if I didn't know, you seem a little...nervous?"

Hades glared at his two brothers. He didn't want to admit that was he was beyond nervous for this; it was bordering on panic.

He had never felt like this, even when Persephone agreed to marry him.

A part of him wondered if the way he was feeling for Katherine was because she was a descedent of Persephone.

No, that couldn't be true. He had felt the same before and after Katherine awoke from Apollo's spell all those months ago. That couldn't be influenced by the fact Katherine was related to his dead wife. It was more than that, deep down he knew that. Katherine was different than Persephone on so many levels.

He knew he wanted this. To have a life with Katherine.

Hopefully she felt the same.

"Now," Zeus smiled. "What do you want us to do?"

Like every morning, Katherine awoke in a cold and empty bed, the only sign Hades was there was the lingering scent of woodpine in the sheets.

Over the last few weeks, he had been avoiding her like the plague. Katherine didn't know why. She never saw him more than a few seconds before he turned down another hall, and before she went to sleep, she would feel the bed dip, letting her know he was there. He would kiss her on the forehead before going to sleep, waking up early and leaving.

Katherine began to worry if Hades was regretting her staying down here in the Underworld. Everything seemed fine to her: she no longer had nightmares, she was getting better at controling her powers with the help of Hecate, and the trials were all in the past.

What was bothering Hades so much?

Sighing, Katherine got out of the comfort of her bed and shuffled to the bathroom to get ready for the day.

When she got out of the bath, she heard someone knocking on the door. Hoping it was Hades, Katherine put on a fluffy robe and hurried to the door.

Instead of Hades, it was her sister Namie. Katherine tried to not let her disappointment show as she smiled and let Namie inside.

She failed to notice the dress in Namie's hands until she saw her sister lay it on the bed.

It was a long and flowy with a modest v-neck and spaghetti straps. It was a pretty peach color with white embrodery on the top. It was the only modern dress Katherine has worn since she arrived those months ago.

"What's with the dress," Katherine asked.

Namie smiled and shrugged, pretending to not know anything. Katherine narrowed her eyes.

"Lord Hades wants you to wear this, and I'll take you to see him."

Katherine's heart leaped when she heard that she would see Hades. Despite being happy to see him after these few weeks, she was also mad that he left her completely alone for no reason, thinking that there was something wrong.

He was going to get a load full from her.

Namie help her sister into the dress before doing her hair and makeup. She kept the hair simple with a sleek and neat high ponytail with the ends slightly curled to give it some wave. She also kept the makeup to a minimum, only doing foundation, mascara and a nude gloss. Namie knew Hades preferred Katherine with little to no makeup.

After the hair and makeup, Katherine slipped on a pair of white ballet slippers instead of heels. The length of the dress covered her feet anyways, so she didn't bother wearing any fancy heel.

Namie gushed as she watched her young sister admire the dress and her look.

At the beginning, she really did have doubts for Hades. She believed him to be a selfish god that would use and disgard her sister. But the way he cared for her during the days leading to the trial and how he put her feelings first, it only proved that he cared for her.

It shocked her when he asked her about what to do with Katherine. It touched her that Hades considered her important to ask Katherine's future with him.

"Ready?"

Katherine looked away from her reflection and nodded. Picking up the front of her dress so she wouldn't trip, she followed Namie, feeling both excited and nervous.

They walked side by side down the hall and into the throne room.

The pews were gone and instead, there were hundreds of gods and goddesses in suits and dresses. They were quiet once they noticed Katherine had stepped into the room. Some were staring at her with hope while others were confused to see her. To many of them, they still thought she was a human. They didn't know about her and Persephone.

She saw Zeus and Posideon standing in front of the crowd with bright smiles on their faces.

"Katherine," Zeus greeted. "It's good to see you well."

"It's good to see you too. If you don't mind my asking, why are you here?"

Zeus smirked, but didn't say anything.

"Does it have to do with Hades?"

"Yes, it does."

Katherine turned to see Hades standing at his throne, wearing a classic black suit and a black crown on his head. She had never seen his crown. The way the shadows swirled and the black crystals glistened in the light.

She felt her beat skip a beat, something that always happened when she saw Hades. He always managed to take her breath away.

Anything in Katherine's mind that told her to tell him off about leaving her vanished when she saw his dazzling smile, her eyes never leaving his as he took each step slowly and carefully towards her. She resisted the urge to run to him.

"I knew that dress would suit you."

"You picked this?" Hades nodded. "It's beautiful. But, why am I wearing it? Why are all the gods and goddesses here?"

"Because... I wanted to ask you something."

Hades pulled a black and velvet box from his pocket and got down on his knee. Katherine's jaw must've dropped to the floor, knowing what he was doing.

"Katherine. I know I was never easy to figure out. I was in a dark place with wounds that refused to heal. I refused to let go of the past, and I was even going to let my being fade to nothing. But when you came along, you intriged me. Despite what you've been through, you still had this sparkle in your eye that refused to die. You were always a mystery when you showed me you danced and played the piano.

"I know I've been avoiding you these last few weeks, but I wanted this to be perfect because you deserve it. I want to make you happy, I want to be the reason you smile instead of cry. I want you by my side, as my wife and queen."

Hades opened the box to reveal a beautiful ring with black diamonds with a pure silver infinity band. Katherine was at a lost of words as she stared at the ring.

"Which brings me to this... Katherine Marie Bakers, would you do me the honor of being my wife?"

He didn't have to ask her twice. Katherine nodded as tears streamed down her face. She smiled when she felt the cool metal of the ring against her finger.

Everyone cheered as the god of the dead embraced his future queen and life. They could see the happiness in his eyes, the smile on his face.

They knew Katherine would make a great Queen. They knew that she was the one meant for Hades.

CHAPTER 27

F our months later...

    To say Katherine was nervous was easy to say the least. Today was her wedding day, a day that she never dreamed of having. Back home, no one saw her, always in Namie's shadow. Even when she died, Katherine shut everyone out. She never expected to be here in a white dress about to get married.

Yet here she was, having servants dress her in a lavous gown, preparing her for her new life.

Queen of the Underworld.

Katherine took a deep breath as someone tightened the corset, causing some of the air to escape her lungs. After a few tugs, the corset was set, leaving Katherine a heaving mess.

"Is a corset really necessary?"

Namie giggled before nodding. "Just remember how to breathe." Katherine groaned.

It took three servants to carry the dress. The dress had a sweetheart neck line with a ball gown skirt that looked three sizes larger than Katherine that pooled at the ends and started a train in the back. It had a lace like pattern embroded into the fabric. The veil had a similar pattern at the edges and flared down to the floor.

It was a beautiful dress. Fit for a queen.

It was a struggle getting the dress on. The skirt itself seemed to weigh a ton. It took all the servants to lift the skirt over Katherine's head. Finally, the skirt was over her head. Katherine breathed in relief as the hard part was over. Namie tightened the bodest and tied it into a bow.

Next was the hair.

Namie twisted and curled her sister's long hair. She tied half of it into a bow shaped bun, leaving the rest of her hair in long black waves. Namie placed the veil onto Katherine's head, using a simple silver comb to clip the veil into the bun.

Namie then went to the makeup. Like at the proposal, she kept the makeup light, only using powder foundation, a nude smokey eye, and a pale pink lipstick.

It was hard for her to not cry as she starred at her sister. She had always dreamed of seeing her sister on her wedding day. Though she was dead, it was still a moment that she was happy to see. Besides, Katherine was not only her sister, but her new queen.

"It's time."

Katherine swallowed the large lump that formed in her throat. She took deep breaths to calm herself, but her nerves were still raging on.

"Don't be so nervous," Namie cooed. "I'll be right next to you the whole time."

"What if I can't do it? What if I'm a bad queen? What if all of the souls start to hate me?"

"You will make an excellent queen. Hades certainly thinks so. We all believe in you, Kat. It's time you believed in yourself as well."

Katherine took a nervous breath before nodding. Namie held her hand, taking note on how her hand shook with nerves.

The halls were silent as they walked closer to the throne room where the ceremony was being held at. All of the Olympic gods and goddesses (Hades' family) and other minor gods were here, waiting for the queen to be.

Hades stood at the alter with Zeus and Posideon, feeling the nerves wash over him the same way they did when he proposed.

It shouldn't have unnerved him. He was married before, he knew how the ceremony went. The bride would first swallow the six pomegranate seeds, accepting the terms set by Demeter when Persephone was alive. Then they would share vows, then the bride would be corronated in front of everyone as the new Queen of the Underworld.

Suddenly, everyone gasped. Hades looked to see Katherine in her dress with Namie by her side. The dress was perfect on Katherine. The smile that was on her face said it all.

He watched her walk down the aisle, oblivious to the stares that everyone sent her. They looked at her in admiration and wonder as they knew she would be an excellent queen.

He smiled when Katherine finally made it to the alter. Namie whispered something to Katherine, making her blush before hugging her sister. After, Namie went into the crowd, leaving Katherine alone.

Hades reached out his hand for her and she gladly accepted it. He pulled her to his side, his smile never leaving.

"You look beautiful," he whispered in her ear.

"You don't look too bad yourself."

Zeus hushed the crowd and soon began with the ceremony. Zeus went over the ceremony of the pomegranates, explaining it carefully to the bride. Katherine nodded, telling him she understood. The god grabbed a small platter beside him and handed them to Hades.

"Since the first winter Demeter casted over the earth, the pomegranate was a symbol for both a fertile harvest and the fruit of the dead. Before returning, Persephone swallowed six seeds from the fruit, allowing her six months out of the year to return home before spending the other half of the year as Queen of the Underworld. By swallowing these seeds, you have rpomised to return every six months to be by my side. Do you accept?"

"I do."

Hades nodded at her, telling her to swallow the seeds. Katherine picked up one and swallowed, grimacing on the slimy and bitter taste they left in her mouth. Hades smiled for her to continue. Katherine swallowd the seeds one by one and soon, she swallowed the last one, glad that it was over. The crowd clapped.

Zeus raised his hand and the crowd was silent.

"We are gathered today to watch the union of Hades, God of the Dead, and Katherine Bakers, desendent of the former queen Persephone," the crowd murmured. "With the pomegranate ceremony completed, both parties will share vows. Hades, repeat after me: I, Hades."

"I, Hades."

"Promise to you Katherine."

"Promise to you Katherine."

"To be by your side in sickness and health."

Hades smiled. "To by by your side in sickness and health."

"To protect you from evil and cherish you as my wife and queen."

"To protect you from evil and cherish you as my wife and queen."

"Until humanity has no use for us gods."

"Until humanity has no use for us gods."

Katherine smiled as tears streamed down her face, no doubt making the mascara run. Zeus did the same for her, asking her to repeat the vows, ands she did gladfully.

"Now, the rings."

A servant stepped forward and handed the couple the rings, both of the bands a beautiful black wedding band, only Katherine's was made out of a black diamond.

"With these rings, they will symbolize your eternal union. The red string of your fates have now been intertwined with each other, a bond stronger that not even the Fates will meddle in."

Hades slipped on the black ring onto Katherine's ring finger, matching beautifully with the silver engagement band. She too slid the black wedding band on Hades hand, feeling the bond that Zeus described flow through her. By the look of wonder on Hades face, he too felt it.

Did he feel the same thing with Persephone?

"By the power of the gods, you are now husband and wife. Now, the coronation."

This was Katherine's moment. Hades stepped aside, leaving Katherine alone with Zeus. She looked at him as her nerves picked up, but he simply smiled encouraging.

Zeus picked up a crystal crown from a servant. The crown was black with crystal sticking out from various places with small pearls and beading embedded into the crown. In the light, it sparkled and glistened with a ray of colors.

The crown symbolized the role that Katherine was about to play. A role to help the dead into their respected afterlives. Was she ready for that responsibilty? Knowing that she might subject a soul to torment for eternaty?

"This crown will symbolize your role as Queen. You will have the power to decide and help souls to their afterlives. You will judge without bias, you will comfort those who are confused, and provide the best solution to the departed. You will be equal to Hades, you will share his burden and duties as a queen. Do you accept the responsiblities as the new Queen of the Underworld, to be fair and just?"

"I do."

She kneeled in front of Zeus, her knees shaking. She felt the weight of the crown on her head, the jaggedness of the crystals.

It was offical.

Katherine was Queen of the Dead.

The crowd cheered and clapped as Hades helped his new wife to her feet, wearing his own crown. The stared at each other in wonder and disbelief, almost like they couldn't believe it themselves.

Hades bent his his forward and placed a soft kiss on Katherine's lips. The kiss was sweet and tender, but held a hidden passion behind it. He pulled away all too soon and took Katherine's hand. They both turned to see the smiles on everyone's face.

Namie was a sobbing mess as she clung to a minor god who looked extremely uncomfortable to say the least. Hades family was among the crowd, all happy to see that their uncle was finally happy after being miserable for so long.

They both deserved to be happy.

EPILOGUE

U nknown POV

I stared at disgust as the newly wed couple danced and laughed as the reception went on. Gods mingled as a small band played music in the corner.

I stayed in the corner, away from everyone, hiding in the shadows. I was surprised to see that none of the gods have noticed my presence yet. Then again, they were always such idiots.

Watching Katherine and Hades dance away made me sick. They were in their own paradise, without a care in the world. I was so close to having Katherine not once, but twice, only to fail. I should've never trusted Apollo with my work.

No matter; that was one god taken care of. And hopefully soon, it will be all of them.

I wanted to see them fall. They locked me away for eons in the dark of Tartarus. I wanted to make them pay. I wanted to kill them all.

If Apollo had succeeded, Katherine would be in my grasp, consumed by the darkness and evil. With her new powers from Persephone and the powers she would uptain as queen, she would be as powerful as Zeus himself. With her by my side, I could overtake the gods and crush Mount Olympus to a pile of rubble.

But I was still too weak. My control over Apollo had consumed most of the energy I gained after my escape.

Hopefully in six months, I would have most of my power back to try and take Katherine from that idiot Hades.

With that final thought, I slipped further into the shadows, disappearing without a trace.

All in good time, my dear Katherine.